# YOU CAN'T HAVE ONE WITHOUT THE OTHER.

Sometimes I worry about getting the Bad Luck. I don't know how you catch the Bad Luck exactly, but I guess it's a lot like catching the stomach flu. Or getting warts. (Truth be told, if you've got the stomach flu AND warts, then your luck probably isn't so good.)

Some people seem to have the Bad Luck an awful lot of the time. Except for my dad being Graveyard Dead and me having an alien for a brother, my luck has been pretty okay up until now. Not real good, but not real bad either. That's the way I like it. Because here's one thing I know about the Bad Luck: It comes right along with the Good Luck. You can't have one without the other.

Which makes me nervous because today has a lot of the Good Luck in it . . .

# OTHER BOOKS YOU MAY ENJOY

# PENELOPE CRUMB
# FINDS HER LUCK

## SHAWN K. STOUT

*with art by* VALERIA DOCAMPO

**PUFFIN BOOKS**
An Imprint of Penguin Group (USA)

PUFFIN BOOKS
Published by the Penguin Group
Penguin Group (USA) LLC
375 Hudson Street
New York, New York 10014

USA * Canada * UK * Ireland * Australia
New Zealand * India * South Africa * China

penguin.com
A Penguin Random House Company

First published in the United States of America by Philomel Books,
an imprint of Penguin Young Readers Group, 2013
Published by Puffin Books, an imprint of Penguin Young Readers Group, 2014

THE LIBRARY OF CONGRESS HAS CATALOGED THE PHILOMEL EDITION AS FOLLOWS:
Stout, Shawn K.
Penelope Crumb finds her luck / Shawn K. Stout ; with art by Valeria Docampo.
pages cm
Summary: Blaming The Bad Luck for not being anyone's Favorite, fourth-grader Penelope Crumb
hopes to change this situation by becoming the lead artist for the mural her class is painting for the
residents of Portwaller's Blessed Home for the Aging.
ISBN (hardcover) 978-0-399-16254-1
[1. Luck—Fiction. 2. Friendship—Fiction.] I. Docampo, Valeria, date – illustrator.
II. Title. PZ7.S88838Pem 2013 [Fic]—dc23 2012048885

Puffin Books ISBN 978-0-14-242637-1

1 3 5 7 9 10 8 6 4 2

*For Anna and Lily*

# PENELOPE CRUMB FINDS HER LUCK

# 1.

Sometimes I worry about getting the Bad Luck. I don't know how you catch the Bad Luck exactly, but I guess it's a lot like catching the stomach flu. Or getting warts. (Truth be told, if you've got the stomach flu AND warts, then your luck probably isn't so good.)

Some people seem to have the Bad Luck an awful lot of the time. Except for my dad being Graveyard Dead and me having an alien for a brother, my luck has been pretty okay up until now. Not real good, but not real bad either. That's the way I like it. Because here's one thing I know about the Bad Luck:

It comes right along with the Good Luck. You can't have one without the other.

Which makes me nervous, because today has a lot of the Good Luck in it:

1. *Mom left for work early.*
2. *Orange Popsicle for breakfast. For real, two.*
3. *Found long-lost T-shirt in rag bag. Still fits except for part that covers my stomach.*
4. *Alien overslept and missed bus.*
5. *Two orange Popsicles in lunchbox. For real, four.*
6. *No surprise test on decimal points.*
7. *Angus Meeker home sick with the stomach flu.*
8. *Not one mean comment about how big my nose is.*
9. *Patsy Cline smiled at me.*

With all that good stuff, I just know that the Bad Luck is right around the corner. But I can't think about corners so much right now because Miss Stunkel is letting us use clay in art class. And so I am busy making a cow.

Patsy Cline Roberta Watson, my used-to-be best

friend, is crazy about cows. Instead of spots like real cows have, I draw hearts in the clay with my pencil point. Just because.

I set the cow on the corner of my desk, so it's as close to Patsy Cline as it can be without jumping over the space between our desks. Patsy Cline is smushing her clay into something that could be a worm that's been run over by a delivery truck. Or else a horse with pneumonia. Patsy Cline isn't so good at art.

I make a *cuuullllggggh* noise with my throat and wait for Patsy to look this way. She does, thank lucky stars, but she has a look on her face that says, You Should Cover Your Mouth.

"Sorry," I say, even though I am really not sorry because it was only a pretend cough and therefore only pretend germs that Patsy doesn't need to be afraid of. "But look." I point to the cow.

When she sees it, her eyes get big and almost weepy and she says, "Oh, how I wish cows had hearts like that in real life."

Which makes me smile.

But then Vera Bogg, who is Patsy Cline's brand-new best friend, crinkles up her teeny nose and says, "But cows *do* have hearts, Patsy Cline."

Good gravy. That's Vera Bogg for you.

With her pink fingernail, Vera presses a smiley face into a small ball and then stacks it on top of two others. "I think it would be better if you made it more like a real-looking cow," Vera says to me, pushing her pink headband back on her head. "And where's its tail?"

I am about to tell Vera a thing or two about art, about Patsy Cline, and about cows, but instead I flatten the cow with my fist. If Vera Bogg doesn't know that art doesn't have to be real-looking, that everybody knows cows have hearts *on the inside,* and that Patsy Cline is allergic to things with tails, then I'm not going to be the one to tell her.

Miss Stunkel walks up and down the rows, and when she gets to my desk, she looks at my flattened cow and says, "Penelope, you've made a pancake? How *nice.*" Only, she says it in a way that makes me think she only eats waffles.

She nods at Patsy Cline's sick horse as she passes, which is now just about dead, and then stops right in front of Vera Bogg. "Oh, Vera," she says. "What a delightful snowman. You're really something." And she makes a big deal out of the *something*.

Vera Bogg's face gets as pink as the rest of her. It's the kind of pink that makes me feel like a raw hot dog. The sort that makes you sick if you don't cook it long enough. Vera Bogg is Miss Stunkel's All-Time Favorite. She'd have to be to get a big-deal *something* for a boring old snowman.

If Mister Leonardo da Vinci was here, he would surely say, "It seems apparent to me, oh me oh my, that Miss Stunkel couldn't tell a craggy rock from a masterpiece." Because that's how dead artists talk.

Then Vera Bogg starts telling Patsy Cline how wonderful Patsy's clay sculpture is, and how she wishes she could make something that good. I can't help but roll my eyeballs. Even Patsy Cline looks a little suspicious, but then she says, "Do you know what it's supposed to be?"

Vera's eyes get wide, and after staring at the lump

on Patsy's desk for a long time, she says, "Well, it looks like it could be a lot of things."

"It's a fiddle," says Patsy Cline.

"That's just what I was going to say," says Vera. "A fiddle."

Patsy Cline nods and smiles, and all I can do is shake my head. Because how Vera Bogg, and not me, can be Patsy's All-Time Favorite is something I will never ever understand.

Meanwhile, I'm molding my pancake into a hungry tiger, which I plan on training to bite at Vera Bogg's ankles, and Miss Stunkel says she has an important announcement so listen up.

A man with a beard that's just on his chin and not on his cheeks comes into the classroom and sits on top of Miss Stunkel's desk. Not in a chair, but on her desk. Which I don't think Miss Stunkel likes too well because she gives him a look that says, Chairs Are Chairs for a Reason.

Miss Stunkel says, "I'd like to introduce you all to Mr. Rodriguez. He is visiting schools in our area to talk about an exciting new art project."

Right away my ears perk up.

Mr. Rodriguez swings his legs and smiles. "Hey," he says. "So, like Miss Stinkel said . . ."

"Stunkel," says Miss Stunkel, and she points her chicken-bone finger at us to make sure none of us thinks that's funny. Even though it very much is the funniest thing ever.

"Sorry, wrong tense," says Mr. Rodriguez, clearing his throat. "Stunkel. Anyway, I'm going all around town to get some volunteers to help with an art project. We're painting a mural at Portwaller's Blessed Home for the Aging."

"Ooh." I drop the tiger and raise my hand high.

Mr. Rodriguez smiles at me, and then Miss Stunkel tells me to hold on and that Mr. Rodriguez is not finished. But I don't need to hear anything else, because I would paint a mural on the moon. On a moon rock. On a MoonPie, even. I, Penelope Crumb, am going to be a famous artist when I grow up, and painting murals is what famous artists do. Just ask Leonardo da Vinci. (Which you could do if he wasn't already dead.)

"The theme of the mural is Mother Goose," says Mr. Rodriguez, "and if you want to do this, you have to show up for the next couple Saturdays and Sundays. So, if you have soccer practice or lunch with Grandma every Sunday, you'll probably have to make other plans." He swings his legs again and smiles. Then he says how it will mean so much to all of the people in the Blessed Home for the Aging and how they don't have so much to live for anymore, seeing how they are so old and almost dead.

Miss Stunkel rubs her Thursday lizard pin and says, "So, if this sounds like something you'd like to participate in, raise your hand."

My hand is still up, but Miss Stunkel is busy looking around the room and writing down the names of other kids on a piece of paper. I stick my other hand in the air and make big circles so she won't miss me. And it works, too, because Mr. Rodriguez points right at me and says to Miss Stunkel, "There's a live one over there."

Miss Stunkel sighs and says, "Penelope Crumb, I've already got your name on the list. So unless you're trying to message Mars, please put your hands down."

Everybody laughs, which makes my cheeks burn. But then Mr. Rodriguez scratches his chin beard and says to me, "I think it's pretty righteous that you're so excited about art."

Righteous. I don't know what that means exactly, but it sounds like he thinks I'm right. Which is something Miss Stunkel never says I am. I smile and give him a look that says, Please Tell My Teacher That She Is Very Wrongeous. And it's a good thing that Miss Stunkel isn't very good at telling what different kinds of faces mean because I would definitely get a note sent home for that one.

That's when Patsy Cline raises her hand and says, "What if you aren't any good at drawing?"

Which really is a surprise. Not because Patsy Cline isn't any good at drawing—she's not—but that she would even want to do an art project at all. Especially on Saturdays and Sundays when her mom makes her practice for singing competitions.

Mr. Rodriguez says, "That's nothing to worry about. And I bet you're better than you think."

She isn't.

Patsy Cline smiles and gives me a look that says, Maybe I'm Not So Bad After All. I put on a smile that says, Well, You're Definitely Not the Worst, Patsy Cline. Because that's the truth. And even if it wasn't, that's the kind of thing you say to your used-to-be best friend. Especially when you'd like more than anything to get her back.

And then I think what good luck this is because now I'll have Patsy Cline all to myself, thank lucky stars. And after she sees me paint, she will surely say, "Penelope Crumb, you are my Favorite, because you are the most wonderful artist, and I was so wrong to throw you over for Vera Bogg, because anybody who wears that much pink can't be right in the head."

But then the Bad Luck peeks out at me from around the corner. Because the next thing I see is Vera Bogg raising her hand.

Maybe it's those pink fingernails, but all I can think of is that I don't want the Bad Luck to get any closer. And the next thing I know, the tiger is in my hand, but only for a second because then it leaps at Vera.

And I have to say, for an untrained tiger, it's pretty good. The tiger knocks her hand down and then hits her desk and falls to the floor. I think its head falls off, poor thing. And Vera screams.

That's when I know the Bad Luck has found me for certain, because Miss Stunkel pulls out her chicken-bone finger and points it at me and says I can be sure she's sending a note home.

# 2.

Terrible practically knocks me over. "Watch out," he says as he swings open the door from our apartment. *He* happens to be the one who isn't watching out, but I decide to keep that to myself because the last thing I need after a day of the Bad Luck is an alien attack.

As he pushes past me toward the stairs, he clips my arm and I drop the note from Miss Stunkel. He drops something, too: a football helmet. And that's when I notice he's got a whole football outfit on. Which doesn't make any sense, because I've been studying my brother real close since he turned into an alien—mostly to make sure he doesn't try to turn me into one, and also to report back to NASA—and if there's one thing I know, it's that aliens don't play sports. At least, this alien doesn't.

"I said watch out," he says just in case I didn't hear him the first time. And he gives me a knuckle punch in my arm.

I rub my arm. "You've got on a football outfit."

"It's a *uniform,* genius. Not an outfit. Don't you know anything?" Then he goes for his helmet, which rolled behind him.

While he's busy doing that, I look for my note. I want to grab it before he can read it and tell me how I'm such a weirdo and how if I get one more note sent home, Mom is going to ship me off to Texas to live with Aunt Renn.

Miss Stunkel's note is by his foot, and I leap on it before he has a chance to snatch it up. I land on his shoes, and his laces poke at my stomach, but I get my note anyway and quick shove it under my shirt.

He hollers my name. And that's when I get hit

with the smell. Aliens have the worst-smelling feet, subway-in-the-summer-smelling feet. Because that's where their brains live. (In their feet, not in the subway.)

"Bluch!" I pinch my nose, but the stink has already half killed me. I know this because I can't feel my hair or eyebrows.

"Get off," says Terrible, trying to shake me off his shoes.

I try to get away, I really do, but now I can't feel my knees.

"Stop playing around!" he yells.

And while I'm down on the floor, I see another note just behind his legs. Which makes me wonder, did Terrible get a note sent home, too? Before I lose feeling in my fingers, I give his bare ankle a pinch, which makes him yell something awful. I shimmy on my elbows through his legs.

Then I grab up the note and turn it over, and I can see his name written in real bubbly, purple ink. Girl-letters. There's even a swirly line underneath with maybe some hearts or smiley faces, but I can't

tell for sure because Terrible yanks the note from my fingers before I can get a real good look.

From the floor, I ask, "Who's that from?" I ask real nicely like we're two friends sitting on a porch swing sipping a glass of mint iced tea. And not like I'm lying here on the floor hoping he won't stomp on me for trying to steal his secrets.

It doesn't work.

Sometimes aliens are smarter than you think.

He says, "You don't want to mess with me." Then he steps over me and tucks the note into his helmet.

Now, it seems to me that keeping a note inside a helmet is a very bad idea because it would do a lot of head-itching. And you can't scratch because of the fact that you have a helmet on your head. And then you are trying to concentrate on making a catch or knocking someone over or whatever you do in football, but you can't because of that itch, thanks to the note that you stuffed up in there.

Plus the fact that a note could fall out of a helmet kind of easy. Like it already did. I tell him all

this, because I am a very helpful-type person, but he gives me another knuckle punch and then disappears downstairs.

I'm still on the floor when Littie Maple finds me. "What's the matter?" she says.

I pull Miss Stunkel's note out from under my shirt and hold it up.

"Oh, Penelope." Littie shakes her head at me. "Not again."

"You don't know what it's like," I tell her. Because Littie is homeschooled, always has been, she's never had to deal with a Miss Stunkel. "She's got it in for me. Because I don't have pink fingernails and make dumb snowmen out of clay."

"Are you talking about your teacher or somebody else?"

"My teacher," I say. "Who else would I be talking about, Littie Maple? My word."

Littie rolls her eyeballs at me. "I was coming over to tell you some news, but it seems like you aren't in the frame of mind to hear anything good."

I sit up. "I could use some good news. Definitely, you know, if it's good."

Littie looks at the ceiling like she's not so sure she wants to tell me. But I know Littie Maple, and she can't hold on to information for very long before it finds a way out. Finally, she gets a look on her face that says, I'm Gonna Burst, and then she squats down beside me and puts both hands on my arm. "There's going to be a new Maple in the family."

"Your momma is letting you get a dog?" I say. "Lucky stars! What kind of dog is it going to be? A big one with lips that drool shoestrings and that curls up right against you under the covers? Can you name it Num-Num?"

"Not a dog," says Littie. "A person. Momma is going to have a baby."

My word. "A baby?"

"That's right."

"What for?" I ask.

"What for?" repeats Littie Maple. "What does anybody have a baby for?"

This is something I don't know, so I ask her this: "Isn't your momma too old to have a baby?"

"I guess not," says Littie. "Anyway, she's not any older than your mom. I'm just saying."

"But my mom isn't having a baby."

Littie puts her hands on her hips. "There are lots of people older than my momma that have babies."

I shrug. "If you say so, Littie Maple." I guess babies are all right. I mean, it's not as good as getting a dog, but still.

"Isn't this the best news?" Littie says.

I give her a look that says, Well, It's Not as Good as Getting a Dog Named Num-Num. Because it isn't.

Littie shakes her head at me.

"Can I name it?"

Littie tells me no way.

"Can I at least call it Num-Num?" I ask.

"No."

"Please," I say.

Littie sighs. "Not to its face, and not in front of me or my parents."

"But at all other times?"

She shrugs. "Okay."

This is good enough luck to get me to my feet. I press the corners of Miss Stunkel's note into my thumbs.

"I've never been a sister before," says Littie, playing with the buckle on her shoe. "I hope the baby likes me."

I tell Littie not to worry and that I've been a sister for some time. "It's real easy. I'll give you lots of pointers."

She nods and gets up. "What does it say?"

I know she means my note, but I pretend I don't, and I don't know why.

"That," she says, pointing to my hand.

I shrug and look at Miss Stunkel's handwriting on the front. "Mrs. Crumb" is what it says, in lines so deep you could get your foot caught in them. I tell Littie that I don't read them anymore because they all say the same thing.

Littie wants to know, "What's your mom going to say about this?"

"Not one thing," I say, stuffing the note back under my shirt.

And when Littie raises her eyebrows at me and says, "What are you going to do with that note?" I get a look on my face that says, I Don't Know What Note You're Talking About, Littie Maple.

# 3.

Grandpa Felix's car smells like potato chips. When I tell him this, he says, "Salt and vinegar or chives?"

I stick my big nose toward the ceiling and draw in the air. "Chives."

He smiles and touches his finger to his nose and then to mine. "Right you are. The Crumb nose never fails."

I look inside the brown paper bag on my lap to check on my paintbrushes and drawing pad.

"We need to get you a better carry-all," he says.

"That's okay."

"Maybe a new toolbox?" He says it real soft like maybe I shouldn't hear it.

I shake my head.

"Right. Too soon," he says. "Too soon."

I nod without looking at him and trace a stain on the bag with my finger. If you squint just right, it looks like a foot that's missing a toe.

When we get to a red light, he pinches my chin. "Let's see what you've got."

I pull out my drawing pad and hold up some of my sketches.

"That's quite a nice hat on Mother Goose you've got there," he says. "And what's she got on her wings?"

"Mittens," I tell him. "You know, because of the fact that old people are close to death and that's why they are cold all the time."

His eyes go wide. "Are they now?"

I tell him that they are, and then pat his arm. Which is covered with a brown cardigan sweater.

"I beg your pardon," he says.

I change the subject. "I've never been to an old

folks' home before. All of the old people I know are either Graveyard Dead or living in Texas. Except for you, Grandpa."

"Just what are you getting at?"

"Not a thing, Grandpa Felix."

"Are you calling me old?"

"No sir," I say. Because if he doesn't know that he's a Golden Oldie, then I'm not going to be the one to tell him.

"What else do you have?"

I show him Jack and Jill, Hey Diddle Diddle, and Down at the Station. Then he starts singing, "Down at the station early in the morning, see the little puff-erbellies all in a row . . ."

The light turns green, but Grandpa is slow to notice until the person in the car behind us beeps his horn a couple of times. "You can go, Grandpa," I say softly.

"I've got it. I've got it." He gets us going again, but not before looking in his rearview mirror and telling the person behind us to not be in such a big hurry. Then he says, "How many times am I driving you to this thing?"

I tell him it lasts for three weekends and hold up three fingers at him.

He shrugs. "I don't know what I'm going to do without my favorite photographer's assistant."

I smile and give him a look that says, I'm Your Only Photographer's Assistant. Then I say, "How many weddings will I miss?"

He holds up two fingers.

"You'll just have to try your best," I say. "Want me to write out a checklist so you don't forget anything?"

Grandpa moves his pointer finger up and down like he's pushing the shutter button on a camera. "You mean there's something else I need to remember besides this?" He says it in a real funny voice that makes me laugh.

"When are you ever going to let me take pictures?" I ask.

"Someday," he says.

"You always say that."

"Then it must be true." He smiles and pulls into the parking lot of Portwaller's Blessed Home for the Aging. "I'll just let you off out front."

"You don't want to come in?" I ask.

He shakes his head. "Can't stomach the smell. Worse than hospitals."

"Oh, right." I slide my drawing pad back into the paper bag.

"I'll pick you up right here this afternoon," he tells me. After I shut the car door and head for the building, he hollers after me, "Be good and don't call anybody old!"

I yell back that I'll try my best, and he pulls away.

Portwaller's Blessed Home for the Aging smells more like flowers than it does a hospital. The kind of flowers that you think might smell nice because they are so pretty, but when you lean in real close and take a deep whiff, you might as well be sticking your nose in a carton of buttermilk. The prettiest flowers sometimes have the worst smell, and I know that's because they spend all their time on their looks.

I, Penelope Crumb, think smelling good is way more important than looks. And it's not just because of my big nose.

Inside the door, there is a lady sitting at a desk who I am careful not to call old. Even though she is a lot. She has a round face with a nose to match and hair that curls out and away from her ears like antlers. She says hello and asks if she can help me.

In a real polite way, I tell her that I don't need any help at the moment, but that I'm here to paint a mural with Mr. Rodriguez and other kids so that all the old people can have something nice to look at. Then I tell her I'm sorry for saying the last part about old people and that I would like to take it back.

She gives me a smile that says, I Don't Mind at All. "You're the first one to arrive, so why don't you have a seat on the couch over there." She points behind her, and that's when I notice that the room we're in looks like somebody's living room, like almost from a real house, with couches and reclining chairs and even a television. Except that it's really clean without sneakers and dirty socks strewn about and there's no one in here. And I wonder if you can still call it a living room even if nobody is really doing much living in it.

I try out the couch for a while, one end and then the other, but then I move to a reclining chair that has a good view of the door. I don't really like to be the first person anywhere, because when I am, I always start to worry that I'm in the wrong place or have got the wrong day or that somebody forgot to tell me that they've changed addresses and here I sit while everybody is someplace else that I don't know where.

With my eyes on the door, I reach into my paper bag and give my paintbrushes a squeeze so that I have something to hold on to. I'm about to ask the lady at the desk if she's sure there hasn't been a call to say that Mr. Rodriguez has gotten into a car accident on the way and almost died but had enough strength to say the words: Portwaller's. Blessed. Home. For. The. Aging. Mural. Cancelled.

Because a cancelled mural is just how the Bad Luck would treat me.

But before I can ask her, a small voice nearby squeaks out, "Give me some candies."

I look around, because if someone is giving out candy, I would like some, too. That's when I see a small woman in a wheelchair beside me. She's pointing her finger at my paper bag.

"Come on," she says. "Don't be stingy now." Her bony arm rests on a hook-latch pillow in the shape of a wiener dog. And there are trinkets, lots of them, hanging by yarn from her chair.

I tell her that I don't have any candies, true blue. And then I pull out my paintbrushes and drawing pad to show. "See?"

She gives me a look that says, I Wasn't Born Yesterday. Which it's easy to see that she wasn't, and I am pretty sure no one would ever think she was. Before I know it, she snatches the paper bag from my lap with her quick, wrinkly fingers. She turns the bag upside down and gives it a shake. When she sees that it's empty, she growls, "Big mistake!"

I'm not sure if she means her or me, but either way she doesn't have to be so shouty about it, I don't

think. Antler Lady behind the desk must agree, because she is on her way over here with her finger pressed to her lips. Somebody is in trouble.

"Nila Wister," she says, and then nods at me, "I see you've met one of the students here to paint a mural in our activity room. Isn't that nice?" Only she says it loud and slow like she's talking to a baby. "Nila is one of our newest residents." Then she gives me a look that says, You'll Have to Excuse Nila, She's Having a Day.

I know this look. My mom gives it to other people when I ask her questions like, "Are you sure you followed a recipe for this meatloaf?" or "Is your hair supposed to look like that?"

Nila rolls her tiny, old eyeballs and says, "The phone's ringing. You better run along and answer it." Antler Lady looks back at her desk, but I don't hear any phone ringing. And she doesn't either because she says, "The phone's not . . ." and then looks down at Nila with slitty eyes. "Behave," she tells her and then goes away.

Now it's just me and this Nila person, because

there's no Patsy Cline, no Mr. Rodriguez, and not even a Vera Bogg to be found. I try to be friendly. "What's wrong with your legs?" I ask.

"My legs?" she says. "You mean other than being ninety-three years old and worn out? Not a darn thing."

"Well, at least you have a nice wheelchair to get around in."

"*Real* nice." Only she says it in a way that I know it's *real* not.

I try again. "Do you like Mother Goose?"

She says no real fast like she keeps the word on the tips of her teeth so that it's ready no matter the question. Do you like rainbows? *No.* Winterberry jam? *No.* Electric blankets? *No.*

Good gravy. I don't know what to say next, so I don't say anything and just watch the door.

I can feel Nila staring at me, but I don't look at her. Instead I decide to pretend she's not sitting beside me, not inching her wheelchair closer. I'm an excellent pretender. But then she pokes at my arm with her finger and says, "How come you don't have candies?"

This is a good question. How come I don't have any candies? My pockets should always be filled with sweets. Orange-flavored ones. Which reminds me, we're out of Popsicles. More of the Bad Luck.

"Well?"

I shrug at her.

She shrugs back at me. "What kind of answer is this?"

I quick try to think of another. "My brother eats them all." Which is not really a lie.

Nila nods in a way that makes me think she might have had an alien for a brother one time. Then she holds up my paper bag, the one she already took from me, and stuffs it behind her back.

"Wait a second . . ."

And then she does something even more worse than that. She reaches her bony little arms over to me and grabs at my paintbrushes. Which I am holding tight in my hands. She pulls, this old lady does (sorry,

Grandpa Felix), and somehow yanks one paintbrush loose. Then she stuffs that behind her back.

"Wait a second!" I say again.

The lady at the desk looks over in our direction, and I put on a face that says, Help, I'm Being Burgled. But don't you know, that lady is an excellent pretender, too. She acts like she doesn't see me, doesn't see that my paintbrush and paper bag have been swiped, and then she is all of a sudden very busy shuffling papers and picking up the phone.

My word.

This is what the Bad Luck can do to you.

# 4.

Mr. Rodriguez and Patsy Cline and Vera Bogg and three other kids I don't know finally show up. And when they do, I tell them about what happened to my paintbrush and paper bag.

None of them believes me. Not even Patsy Cline.

"Are you sure that's what happened?" she says to me. "Maybe you just forgot them at home."

Like I made up the whole thing about Nila Wister and her grabby fingers.

Even Vera Bogg can't help herself. "Why would an old lady take your paintbrush?" she says.

The Bad Luck is why. I tell her not just my paintbrush is what I said, and that she also took my paper bag with a foot-stain on it. And then I say, "Vera Bogg, you shouldn't call somebody old. It's very rude."

Her face turns a little pinker and then she says she's sorry. Patsy Cline's face goes a little pink, too. Probably because she's embarrassed to have such a friend.

After giving us name tags, Mr. Rodriguez tells us to follow him. He leads us down a long carpeted hall, and on the way we pass ten or so old people in wheelchairs just sitting there in the hallway for I don't know why. I smile at them and try not to stare, which is hard to do because 1) it's not every day you see so many people doing nothing but sitting in a hallway, and 2) some of them are staring back.

We follow Mr. Rodriguez into an activity room where the residents (he means old people) play games, he says. There are shelves filled with games—Regular non-old-people-type games—like checkers, Parcheesi, Old Maid. On the other side of the room, there's a small kitchen with white cupboards. The whole place seems like it wants you to forget that you're in a nursing home, which you could probably do if you didn't have to live in a nursing home.

Mr. Rodriguez pats his hand against the only empty wall in the room. "This, my artist friends, will be our canvas," he says.

The most wonderful sight in the world: a blank wall. I can practically hear Mister Leonardo da Vinci say, "Pray tell, my dear girl, what are you waiting for? A mural awaits."

I set down my other paintbrushes and drawing pad on one of the tables in the center of the room and pull my No. 2 Hard drawing pencil from my back pocket. As soon as my pencil point touches the wall, my hand starts to move.

Mother Goose's beak is halfway done when somebody yells, "Look! She's starting already! No fair!"

It takes me a couple of seconds before I realize they are talking about me. And when I stop my hand and turn around, everybody is crowded around me, staring. My ears start to sweat.

"Somebody is really anxious to get going," says

Mr. Rodriguez, scratching his chin beard. He leans in to have a look. "You've even given her glasses."

"Mother Goose has a hard time seeing things," I explain. "Because of, well, because she's been around for a while." I'm real careful not to say the O word.

"I see," he says. "You've given this some thought."

I nod.

"What else have you thought about for the mural?"

I point to my drawing pad on the table, and Mr. Rodriguez flips through it. He doesn't say anything, and I don't say anything. And everybody else doesn't say anything. And the room is quiet except for the turning of pages, so quiet you can hear the squeak of a wheelchair as it rolls past the door. I look to see if it's Nila Wister because maybe I could get my stuff back.

It isn't.

Mr. Rodriguez gets to the last page of my drawing pad and then closes it up. "These are really wonderful," he says in front of everybody. "Very inspired and impressive, especially for someone your age."

He goes on and on, using words I don't know but that sound good, and the more he talks, the more my face gets hot.

All the other kids are looking at me, and I feel big all of a sudden, Thanksgiving Day Parade Balloon big. I'm taking up too much space in the room, so much that I worry parts of me might spill out through the windows. And as Mr. Rodriguez keeps on talking about my drawings, I want to shrink and disappear into the empty wall. I wonder if this is how Vera Bogg feels when Miss Stunkel says she is really *something*.

Finally he stops talking and asks the other kids what they think about using my drawings for the mural. Vera Bogg is the first one to say no. And when she does, I'm regular size again, maybe smaller.

Vera says she thinks that Mother Goose should be wearing a pink dress and holding a parasol. The kid with the name Marcus says instead of Mother Goose we should do an outer-space theme with robots and laser guns. A girl named Birgit wants there to be unicorns and rainbows. Alexander wants to make

Humpty Dumpty into a car that falls off a cliff. Patsy Cline asks if there can be just cows.

Then instead saying no to everyone, instead of saying, "There will be no robots or guns or crashing cars or rainbows or just cows," Mr. Rodriguez says that this is a group art project and that he's not in charge.

"But you're the teacher," says Vera Bogg. "Who's in charge if you aren't going to be?"

I hold my breath because what if he says that Vera Bogg is in charge? What if everything turns pink?

Instead, Mr. Rodriguez says that we all have to decide as a group and work together. Which is a real bad idea. Because for the next hour, Mr. Rodriguez sits in a corner of the room reading a magazine while Alexander and Vera Bogg argue about whether or not Jill pushed Jack and why is the water all the way up a hill anyway? Miss Stunkel never lets us be on our own, and this must be why.

Mr. Rodriguez interrupts just to say that we only have three weekends to finish the mural so less arguing and more drawing. "You can elect a leader among you, if you are having trouble deciding what to do as a group, you know."

I can practically hear Mister Leonardo say, "Thank lucky stars, a democracy saves the day! Remove yourself from the background at once, little darling, and for heaven's sakes let's see some art."

"I think we should vote," I say.

Everybody looks surprised to see me, like they've forgotten I am here.

"Vote on what?" asks Marcus.

"On who should be the Boss," I say.

"I agree," says Vera Bogg. "We'll go around, and everybody say who you want to be in charge. "Patsy Cline, you go first."

Patsy Cline looks like she's just been attacked by something with a tail. She chews on her thumb and then looks at her feet. After a long while, she whispers, "I vote for Penelope."

Well then. The surprise almost makes me go dead. The pink disappears from Vera's face like she's just been pushed down a hill.

The rest of the kids vote for themselves. Which

works out real good for me, because I already have a vote, thanks to Patsy Cline. And once Vera Bogg votes for Vera Bogg, all I have to do is vote for me and then I'm the winner, thank lucky stars.

"Your turn," Birgit says to Vera.

Vera opens her eyeballs wide at Patsy Cline and then at me, and I wonder how long it will take Vera Bogg to say her own name. It takes a lot longer than I thought, because Vera never does say her own name. Instead, one corner of her pink mouth turns up and she finally says, "I vote for Patsy Cline."

I hold on to the edge of the table. Miss Stunkel is right, this Vera Bogg really is something. I'm no good at math, but I know enough to know that because of Vera Bogg, I'm going to lose no matter what. Because of Vera Bogg, now I have to decide between me and my used-to-be best friend.

"It's a tie, so far," says Alexander. "One vote each." He points to me. "You're the tiebreaker."

"She's going to vote for herself," says Marcus. "It's over."

"She could vote for anyone," says Vera Bogg. "It's all up to Penelope."

This is when I know that the Bad Luck has its arm around my neck and isn't letting go. Because if I don't vote for Patsy Cline, I might never get her back. I might never be her Favorite again. And if I do pick her, well, Patsy Cline doesn't know anything about art. And why would you make somebody like that the Boss?

Patsy Cline is biting her thumb hard.

If this was some kind of country-western singing group, I'd want Patsy Cline to have the lead part, wouldn't I? And besides all that, Patsy Cline voted for me. She did! I heard her. She said, "I vote for Penelope." Just like that. She must want me to be in charge. And if I go against what she wants, I'll never be her Favorite again.

Mister Leonardo whispers in my ear, "Whatever are you waiting for, my dear?"

"Vote already," says Marcus.

So I do. "Me," I say. "I vote for me."

# 5.

I'm the Boss. And now everybody is waiting for me to tell them what to do. Which is hard, because I just don't know, seeing how I've never been a Boss before.

Patsy Cline won't look at me for some reason. Vera Bogg won't stop looking at me, and I really wish she would.

"What about my outer-space idea?" says Marcus.

Alexander says, "What about monster trucks?"

I give them both a look that says, When Was the Last Time You Saw Mother Goose on a Monster

Truck? And then because I can see Marcus and Alexander aren't so good at telling what different kinds of faces mean, I say, "When was the last time you saw Mother Goose on a monster truck?"

Alexander scratches his head like he's trying to remember. And the next thing I know, everybody is talking about what they want in the mural and isn't the Boss supposed to be the decider? I look to Mr. Rodriguez for help, and finally he puts down his *Art Now* magazine and says, "Why don't you each draw out what you'd like the mural to look like, so Penelope can see." Then he says he needs to step out for a minute but will be back.

I tear blank pages from my drawing pad and hand them out. Everybody gets busy with the drawing, and because I'm in charge, I do what Miss Stunkel does: walk around and judge everybody's work.

It's bad. And I'm not just saying that because I'm trying to be like Miss Stunkel. Which I would never want to be—because, well, her finger for starters. I'm saying it because it's real true. Marcus won't give

up on his spaceships. Alexander isn't drawing at all. Instead, he has written in big angry letters: IF WE CAN'T HAVE TRUCKS, I QUIT! Birgit is covering her drawing with her arms and doesn't want me to see. Patsy Cline is drawing something, but I can't tell what because it's the size of a flea. She tells me she's one hundred percent certain it's not a flea, though. And then she looks mad at me for asking twice.

To my surprise, Vera Bogg is not drawing a snowman. She is drawing a girl in a frilly dress with ribbons and a wide, lacy hat. There's a sheep, too. With ruffles. Vera catches me looking and then explains that she's drawn Little Bo Peep but the sheep isn't lost just yet. She says that if the sheep was lost and wasn't in the mural, nobody would know that Little Bo Peep was Little Bo Peep. They might think she was Mary Had a Little Lamb. Which is a whole other Mother Goose rhyme altogether. "And it wouldn't be right to confuse the elderly."

I'm about to give her a look that says, You Make

My Head Hurt, Vera Bogg, when I see Nila Wister roll by the door in her wheelchair.

Maybe it's because I've been voted the Boss and am on my way to be a not-dead famous artist, but all of a sudden I feel brave. "Keep drawing," I tell everyone. "I'll be right back."

I follow Nila Wister down the hall. Past the people in their wheelchairs, who are still just sitting as far as I can tell, and as I hurry by, I can feel their eyeballs on me and I feel bad all of a sudden for having legs that work and for not being old like them.

My feet don't go as fast as Nila's wheels do, so I don't catch up with her until the nurse rolls her into a room. The door is open, but I knock anyway because being polite is the first step in getting your stuff back.

Nila has her back to the door and says, "I don't need any more pills. Go away." She waves her arm, and when she does, the trinkets on her wheelchair swing.

"I don't have any pills," I say. "Or candies. Or any more paintbrushes or bags." I say the last part just in case she has plans to steal something else of mine. She turns her ancient neck to look at me, and when she sees me, she doesn't invite me in. But she doesn't say, "Go away, you're as unwanted as a warty toad," either. So I take a step inside.

The walls in Nila's room are covered in posters. Carnival posters of elephants and clowns and people in old-timey outfits diving into water. There's even one of a strongman, with giant muscles, so strong he's lifting a planet over his head. One poster has a Ferris wheel in it, and a roller coaster. And above her dresser, there's one of a lady with a scarf tied around her head and big hooped earrings. There is something about this lady, something I've seen before, but I don't know what.

"What are all these?" I ask.

Nila looks at me sideways and then at the posters. "Mine."

This is something Terrible would say. "I know they are yours," I tell her. "But I mean, what do you have them all for?"

"My life," she says.

I don't know what she means exactly because what does her life have to do with a bunch of posters from a carnival? I stare at the muscle-y man and wonder if his arms ever get tired of holding up that world. I can almost see him wink at me as he answers, "Only when it rains, little darling."

The bottom of some of the posters have the words "Coney Island" on them. "Is that where ice cream cones are made?" I ask.

Nila frowns. "That some kind of joke?"

I shake my head. "Nope. I never joke about ice cream."

"Me neither."

"That's a real place then?" I say. "Coney Island? Because it sounds made up."

Nila flaps her lips and then tells me that if I plan on sticking around, I should come stand in front of her so she won't get a stiff neck, or else I should turn her chair. I grip the handles of her wheelchair and pull her toward me and around until she's facing me. When I do, she says, "That's better," and then, "It's a dream."

I don't know if that means Coney Island is a real place or it isn't. So I tell her about a dream I had once that we lived in a house, not an apartment but a real house, and it was made out of cotton candy. "The whole thing," I tell her. "The walls, the roof, the couch, the refrigerator, the fireplace, the beds, the pillows, the dishes . . ."

"I get the idea," says Nila.

"Well, every time I tried to go into a different room, I'd sink into the floor. You know, because even the floor was made out of cotton candy. Just like the walls and the roof and the couch . . ."

She rolls her eyeballs at me, I don't know what for. Then she says, "Is that all?"

"Pretty much," I say. "I woke up after I ate the shower curtain."

She says, "Humph," and then nothing else.

"Is Coney Island really like that?" I ask.

She nods. "Even better."

"Then how come you're here?" I say. "I would never leave a place like that."

She gives me a look that says, You Don't Know

Anything, Little Girl. And then she says, "Why are you here?"

"To paint a mural down the hall, remember?" I say it real nice because it's not her fault that she's old and doesn't remember things. "I've been elected the Boss, sort of."

"No," she says. "Why are you *here?*"

Oh. I quick do a search for my stuff. "I wanted to know if you are done with my paintbrush. And my bag."

She shakes her head.

I say, "I think you took them by mistake." Sometimes you have to lie to be nice when you are trying to find stolen property.

"You got any candies?" says Nila.

I tell her no.

Then Nila Wister looks me right in the eyeballs and screws up her tiny mouth. She says, "Then I'm not done."

Good gravy.

"When do you think you will be done?" I say.

"When do you think you will have some candies?"

"Maybe tomorrow?" I say, hoping this is the right answer.

Nila waves her hand at me like she wants me to go. "We'll see," she says.

On my way out, I look again at the poster of the lady with the scarf. There are words in fancy letters above her head: "If You Wish to Find Which One Is True, It Is the Fortune Lady Who Will Tell It to You." The look in the lady's dark eyes says, I Will Tell You Your Dreams. And that's when I know.

"That's you," I say, pointing. "You are the Fortune Lady?"

Nila flaps her lips at me. Which I take to mean, Yes Indeedy, I Am.

"What kinds of fortunes do you tell?" I ask. "Good or bad ones?"

"You can't have one without the other," she says. Then before I know it, she fixes her eyeballs on me like she's looking deep inside, seeing things that I don't know are there. She looks at me so long and so hard that I think she could even beat Patsy Cline in a staring contest. Finally, when I think she might have gone to sleep with her eyes open or maybe even died, she says, "You've lost something."

Some fortune lady she is. I put my hands on my hips. "My paintbrush and bag. Which you already know because you took them."

Nila Wister rolls her old, dark eyeballs at me. Then she tells me to hush and that she's not talking about my dumb old paintbrush or bag. She blinks at me a couple of times, and says, "You've lost *someone*."

I gulp.

"And that's not all."

"What's not all?" I ask.

"There's trouble about."

"About what?"

"You," she says.

I whisper, "The Bad Luck."

"Yes," she says, sniffing the air, "I can smell it."

I don't say anything. Because what do you say to a Fortune Lady who can see inside you? Who knows what you know, but more of it. And who can smell the Bad Luck. I stick my big nose in the air and sniff, too. But all I can smell is arthritis cream, the same kind Grandpa Felix uses.

"Are you sure?" I ask.

"You don't smell it?" She looks at my big nose and then raises one eyebrow at me, disappointed.

I sniff again and shake my head. "What does the Bad Luck smell like?"

But before Nila can answer, a nurse comes into the room and says it's time for lunch.

"I'm not hungry," Nila growls.

"Oh, Ms. Wister, don't be such a grump," says the nurse. "You've got to eat." My stomach rumbles, and the nurse must hear it because she looks at me and says, "Who's your little friend?"

"Nobody," I say quickly, heading for the door. But before I go, I say to Nila, "Does it smell like fried onions?" Because if I was the Bad Luck, that's what I think I would smell like.

Nila raises her eyebrows at me. Which I know means, Yes, as a Matter of Fact, It Does. And then

I race down the hall toward the activity room, my nose searching the air for any sign of the Bad Luck. On the way, a smell stops me cold for a second, but thank lucky stars, after a couple of more sniffs, I know it's just the spaghetti and meatballs from the dining room.

When I get to the activity room, something stinks like pink. Vera Bogg has got a big smile on her face. She says, "Penelope, you're back. While you were gone, we voted again."

She says it like I've been gone for a gazillion years, like they all thought I was dead and now have moved on with their lives and can barely remember some girl with a big nose who might have been in charge a long, long time ago.

"But I was only down the hall," I say.

"Still."

"But I'm the Boss," I say, wishing I had my clay tiger with me. Vera's ankles could use a good bite.

"We know," she says, "but you were gone, and we needed to decide something and there was no-body here to do it."

I tap Patsy Cline on the shoulder. "Where's Mr. Rodriguez?"

She says in a soft voice, "Wrangling up our lunch."

"What was the vote?" I ask.

Vera Bogg says that they decided that everybody's ideas should be in the mural. Even the monster trucks. Then she tells me that since I'm the Boss it's my job to make them Mother Goosey. She hands me the drawings they did while I was gone. Monster trucks, spaceships, unicorns, and asteroids. I can't look at any more.

If Mister Leonardo was here, he would surely say, "You have been cursed for certain, and you must find a way to break it before your beloved masterpiece is ruined."

And he would be right.

# 6.

I tap my No. 2 Hard drawing pencil against my head to get my brains going. On Regular days, this usually works. But today is no Regular day.

I pull my feet underneath me on the couch and curl myself up real small so that my brains don't have to think about what my arms and legs are doing and can concentrate on my problems.

Mom says, "There is no such thing as bad luck," when I tell her about the mural and Nila Wister and that if we had some sweets around the apartment every once in a while, things might not be so bad. Oh, and that we're out of orange Popsicles again.

Then she tells me that she was in my room earlier today and what a mess. "I don't know how you can find anything in there, and I want you to clean it," she says.

I tell her I will, I will, and then get back to tapping.

All she can do is shake her head at me, and before she heads down the hall, she says, "You're going to hurt yourself."

I don't pay any attention and keep on with the tapping until my pencil slips and gets me in my eyeball. "Ow."

"Told you," Mom calls from the other end of the apartment.

"See?" I say, rubbing my eye. "And you say there's no such thing as the Bad Luck."

Littie Maple comes in just then and sinks beside me on the couch. She's got a notepad and a pen in her lap. And she doesn't turn on the TV like she always does, so I ask her what's wrong.

"Nothing." She looks down the hall. "Pretend I'm not here."

That's pretty easy to do, especially when I'm trying to get my brains to start working good on a plan. I flip through the bad drawings the rest of the group did while I went to get my paintbrush and bag back from the Fortune Lady.

"What are those?" asks Littie.

"I thought I'm supposed to pretend you aren't here."

"Right," she says. "You are. I'm not." Then after a while she says, "Is your brother home?"

I put down the drawings. "Littie Maple, for somebody who isn't here, you sure do ask a lot of questions."

"Well, is he?"

I tell her that he's at football practice but should be home soon. "What do you want with him anyway?"

"I want to observe you," she says. "You know, how you are with each other. Since you're a sister, and I'm going to be a sister, too, when the baby gets here. I'm just saying."

"Do I have to talk to him?" I ask.

"Nope. Just act regular." Littie crisscrosses her

legs at end of the couch and has her pen ready. "I'll be just like Jane Goodall in the Gombe Stream Valley."

"Who?"

"The woman who lived with the chimps in Africa," says Littie. "You know, the scientist." And then she gives me a look that says, Don't You Know Anything?

I give her a look right back that says, Are You Calling Me a Monkey?

She shakes her head and whispers, "I'm. Not. Here."

I tell her okay if she wants to do a science experiment, but that being a sister to an alien is a lot different from being a sister to a normal baby. Just so she knows.

She says she knows, she knows, and then tells me to stop talking.

My word. I stare at Patsy Cline's drawing of the thing that looks like a flea but isn't, according to her.

After a while Littie says, "Do you think he'll be much longer? Momma wants me back for supper in an hour."

"Some scientist you are, Littie Maple. Telling me

to be quiet and then asking me questions the whole time. You're lucky I'm not a monkey or I'd run up a tree to get away from you."

"Well, I can't really do much observing if he's not here, can I!" she says. "And they were chimpanzees, not monkeys. I'm just saying."

I put my pencil and the drawings on the coffee table. "Since you know so much, here's a question for you: Do you think there is such a thing as the Bad Luck? Because I do."

Littie's eyes get big. Then she puts a finger over her lips and whispers, "Don't."

"Don't what?"

"Don't say those words," she says, shaking her head.

"You mean the Bad Luck?"

She squeals and leaps at me, covering my mouth with her hand. "Shhhh. You might as well deliver an engraved invitation on a pillow."

"So you do believe." This is a surprise because Littie Maple has never seemed to be a good- or bad-luck kind of thinker. She always sees things just as they are and not how they should be. "Do you know how to get rid of it?" I ask.

"I think it has to decide to go away on its own," she says softly. "Or maybe you could help it along with a charm."

Thank lucky stars for Littie Maple. "A good-luck charm," I say. "Like a horseshoe or something?"

She nods. "Can we talk about something else now? All this talk about You Know What is giving me a nervous stomach. And Momma is making pasta Bolognese for supper."

I give her a look that says, What Does That Have to Do with the Price of Peas? And she says that her momma's cooking has gotten a lot better since she's been taking a cooking class, that's all.

I tell her fine and I'm about to ask her if she knows where I can get my hands on a horseshoe when the door to our apartment swings open. It's Terrible. And right behind him, not more than a couple of inches away from him, there's a girl. A real live one. Littie and me look at each other with our mouths hanging open because we didn't think Terrible knew any girls. And even if he does, I didn't think any girl would ever want to know him.

He gives me a sideways look. But it's so quick I'm not sure I really saw it, because the next thing I know he's got a big smile on his face, so big I can see most of his pointy, alien teeth. "This is my baby sister, Penelope," he tells the girl in a voice that's so full of sugar that my cheeks pucker. "And Leticia Maple. She lives across the hall."

I want to roll my eyeballs at him for the baby remark, but there's no time because Littie's face is scrunched up small and she's turning red all over. Littie doesn't let anybody call her by her real name, and with a name like Leticia, I don't blame her one bit. I quick grab her arm because I know she wants to jump up and bend Terrible's fingers back until he says sorry. I could let her, but it's never a good idea to get in a finger fight with an alien. Especially when the Bad Luck is floating around.

Littie shakes me off and then grabs her pen and starts stabbing at her notebook. I can only imagine what she's writing.

Terrible doesn't seem to notice Littie's new red color or her murdering scribbles. He points his thumb at the girl standing next to him and says, "This is Tildy."

Littie's scribbles get louder, and I worry that there are tears filling up her eyeballs. So I say, "Hey, scientist lady, you're going to scare away all of the monkeys making that racket." Then I swing my arms over my head, bend my legs, and circle the coffee table howling like a monkey. Then I monkey-wave at the Tildy girl and announce that I'm not a baby and Littie's name is Littie. And that Terrible is just showing off for her.

This works because Littie stops with the stabbing and almost smiles. Then she starts writing regular in her notebook, probably about how good I am at being both a monkey and a sister at the same time.

Tildy looks at my alien brother and says, "Did she just call you Terrible?"

Now Terrible gives me a sideways look for sure. But before he has a chance to clobber me, I grab up the drawings and pull Littie into my room.

# 7.

Littie and me make horseshoes out of construction paper. Hers looks more like a *V*, truth be told, but when I tell her so, she shrugs and says, "Not every horse has a perfectly round foot. I'm just saying."

"Do you want me to make a horseshoe that actually looks like a horseshoe for you instead?" I ask. Because that *V* has an awful big corner in it, and corners are just where the Bad Luck likes to hide.

She tells me no, and then she says she just remembered she has to go home to help her mom pick out colors for the new baby's room.

"I'll help," I say, seeing how I'm the one who's the artist. And it's an artist's job to know about colors.

"That's okay," says Littie.

"At May's Hardware, you can get little pieces of paper with paint colors on them for free. And you don't even have to ask, you can just take them," I tell her. "For free. Only you have to leave one or two of each, because if you take them all and don't leave any for paying customers, Mr. May will yell at you and tell you to never step foot in his store again, you blasted thief. But I know for a fact that Mr. May doesn't work on Thursday nights. I'll get some good colors for you."

"That's okay," she says again. "My momma probably already has some."

"But are they *good* ones?" I ask. "Because you don't want bright oranges or reds, you know. Num-Num shouldn't wake up every day thinking he's being grilled like a kabob."

Littie shakes her head at me. "I think I know enough about colors to know we aren't going to have room that looks like it's on fire."

"Okay, Littie Maple," is all I say because if she thinks she knows as much about colors as she does about horseshoes, which isn't much at all, I'm not going to be the one to tell her any different.

After Littie leaves, I string my horseshoe around my neck and get back to the drawings. Being the Boss sure is hard. Especially when you want the mural you're in charge of to be not-bad-looking. But now that I have my horseshoe, all I have to do is wait for the Good Luck to find me and give me an idea.

I look at Patsy Cline's drawing of something that isn't a flea one more time. Whatever it is, at least it's small enough to go anywhere that nobody would even notice.

"Brilliant thinking," Mister Leonardo would certainly say. "The flea could ride under a goose feather, or perhaps even in Mother Goose's fine bonnet, and no one would be the wiser."

"But what about the rest of the drawings?" I say. "A monster truck can't be flea-size." And there's Vera Bogg's pink Little Bo Peep and matching sheep. "Who ever heard of a pink sheep anyhow?" And

Marcus's spaceship, and everything else that doesn't belong in Mother Goose.

"A stiffened spine. That's what it takes," Mister Leonardo would say. "No matter how much she may have begged, I could have never painted my dear Mona Lisa in an Ornithopter Flying Machine. I would have been laughed out of Italy had I agreed."

My word. If I'm ever going to be a non-dead famous artist, I can't be laughed out of Portwaller's Blessed Home for the Aging. Or anyplace else. Mr. Rodriguez would take back all those nice things he said about me, and Patsy Cline wouldn't take me back ever.

I stare at Alexander's monster truck for a long time, so long that I imagine loading it with Marcus's spaceship, Patsy Cline's tiny non-flea, Birgit's sparkly rainbow unicorns, and all of Vera Bogg's pink and then driving them to the moon, where they can be in their own bad-looking mural that I'm not the Boss of. And that only the Man on the Moon has to see.

I lay the drawings on the floor next to my bed and

before I go to sleep, I pat my horseshoe and ask for the Good Luck to come.

I'm up early the next morning looking for sweets for the Fortune Lady. I check all the cupboards, but I guess the Good Luck must be busy hanging around somebody else's horseshoe and didn't hear me invite it over because, like always, there are no sweets in the house. No candies, no cookies, no jelly doughnuts even.

I leave a note for my mom on the refrigerator because maybe Mom will pay attention more than the Good Luck:

Missing:
ORANGE POPSICLES! and other tasty treats.
Last seen: Hardly ever.
If you know how to get some, tell Penelope.

In the meantime, the best I can do is make my own sweets, so I grab the honey jar from the cupboard and pour some into a bowl. I spoon in a bunch of sugar, all that we have, stirring it up real good. Then I load it onto a celery stalk. Which is the only thing I can think of to put it on and also because I, Penelope Crumb, like sweet things when they have a nice crunch. I stuff the celery into a paper lunch bag and wrap the end with a thick rubber band.

"What have you got there?" asks Grandpa Felix when he picks me up.

"Crispy Sticky," I tell him, holding up the paper bag. Because all sweets taste better if they have a name.

"Well, it's leaking all over my seat," he says.

"Oh, sorry." I wipe the spill with my finger and stick it in my mouth. Then I cup my other hand around the bottom of the paper bag, which is now pooling with honey.

Grandpa Felix gives me a sideways look that says, You Better Do Something with That Mess, Pronto. So I put down my window and let Crispy Sticky leak onto the road. Grandpa sighs but he doesn't say he's pulling over to a gas station for me to dump that mess in the garbage where it belongs, so I change the subject.

"Do you like my horseshoe?" I say, looking down at the paper charm hanging around my neck. "Littie and me made them last night."

He nods. "I do. But it's upside down, you know."

"What do you mean?"

"It's bad luck that way," he says. "The open part should be facing up to the sky so that you can catch all the good luck that comes down." He holds up his fingers in a U-shape. "Like this. The way you have it now, the good luck will spill right over."

"Good gravy!" Still holding Crispy Sticky out the window, I pull at the string around my neck. But the honey on my hand sticks in my hair at the back of my neck, and I can't get the knot untied.

Grandpa says, "Wait until we get there and I'll help you."

But I can't take a chance on the Bad Luck seeing my upside-down horseshoe. If it does, it will probably think I want it to hang around me, that it's my new Favorite thing. So I flip the horseshoe right side up so that it will catch the Good Luck in its belly. But when I try to pull my hand away, the honey sticks and so do my fingers.

I holler.

"What's the matter now?" says Grandpa, trying to keep his eyeballs on the road so he doesn't crash into a parked car and kill us dead.

I can't get any words out because my brains can only think about my sticky fingers on the paper horseshoe and what to do about that. My brains don't have to think about that too long, though, because there's a bump in the road and Grandpa Felix drives right over it. And if there's one thing I'm sure of, it's that the Bad Luck put that bump there because as soon as we hit that bump 1) I drop Crispy Sticky, and 2) my honey fingers come unstuck, taking half of the horseshoe with them.

Well then.

Grandpa parks the car in front of Portwaller's Blessed Home for the Aging and turns to me. "You couldn't wait?"

I shake my head. Because if I could've, I would still have a sweet for the Fortune Lady plus a good-luck charm.

He says, "Whatever you do, don't you touch anything. I'm coming around to let you out." He gets out of the car and opens my door for me. Then he tells me to go straight inside to the bathroom and wash my sticky hands. He doesn't tell me good-bye, or to have a good day, and his words have rocks in them. And when I say, "Grandpa, I'll remember not to call anybody old today," hoping for a smile or maybe a laugh, he just sighs at me and gives me a look that says, Your Antics Are Aging Me Fast.

# 8.

Nila Wister is waiting for me just inside the door. "Give me some candy," she says.

I hold up my honeyed hands and tell her that I tried but Crispy Sticky is lying along the side of the road somewhere between here and our apartment. This is the kind of Bad Luck day I'm having.

She flaps her lips and says, "Big mistake." Then she stares at me again, looking for I-don't-know-what deep inside. I worry that she's going to tell me something I don't want to know, something bad, something about losing someone or being all alone as nobody's

Favorite. But after a long time of looking, she blinks her eyes and says, "What's that around your neck?"

I tell her it's a broken horseshoe, and she says, "Like I said, trouble all around you, girl."

This isn't so good to hear from a Fortune Lady. She fidgets, and the trinkets on her wheelchair swing.

"What do I do?" I ask. "About the trouble."

"Not much you can do about trouble except stand up to it," she says. "Look it in the eye and show it who's boss."

"I am the Boss," I tell her. "I mean, of the mural, anyway."

Nila says, "Humph." And then, "If you're *really* the boss, then you shouldn't have any trouble." It comes out like she doesn't believe I'm the Boss. And maybe I don't believe it much either.

I point to the trinkets tied to her wheelchair with strands of yarn. "What about those?"

"What about them?" she says.

"Are they for luck?"

She nods.

"Where did you get them?"

Nila Wister brushes her tiny fingers against each one. An acorn, a set of keys, a glass figurine in the shape of a butterfly, a horseshoe. "My father."

Oh. Then I tell her that my father is Graveyard Dead and that the only thing I have of his is a shoe-horn.

She nods like maybe she knew that already, seeing how she is a Fortune Lady and all. And then she tells me something else. "I'm here because my sister lived in Portwaller, and she was taking care of me."

"I don't have a sister," I say. "I have a brother. And he's an alien."

"I had one of those, too," she says, shaking her head.

I don't know if she means a brother or an alien, but by the look on her face I figure probably both. "Where is she now?" I say. "Your sister, I mean."

Nila Wister points to the ceiling, and because there's no upstairs in Portwaller's Blessed Home for the Aging, I know she means she's Graveyard Dead.

I tell her I'm sorry, and she says that it's neither here nor there. But it must be somewhere close by, be-cause her eyes get watery. And then all of a sudden she clears her throat and says, "That's the sorriest horseshoe I've ever laid eyes on."

"I made it last night, but it didn't live very long," I say, eyeing the honeyed, half-torn paper strip.

"You can't make a charm out of just any old thing like paper," she tells me. "The only thing you get is paper cuts." Nila fingers her keys. Then she leans in close. "I suppose you want to borrow one of mine."

My eyes get big. "Could I?"

"No."

Well then.

"Charms are particular," she says. "No guarantee they'll work for you. You might have to just find your own."

"What about a four-leaf clover? Maybe I could find one of those."

Nila Wister bats her hand in the air. "Never did find them to be very lucky."

A nurse comes down the hall and tells Nila that it's time to get her hair washed. Nila groans. "I don't want it cut," she says to the nurse. "The last time, that girl used hedge trimmers on me. I looked like some kind of juniper."

The nurse laughs and shakes her head as she pushes Nila in her chair down the hall. Before they disappear around a corner, Nila waves her hand and yells something about trouble.

"Penelope," calls Mr. Rodriguez from behind me. "Come on, I've got some exciting news to share."

I'm the last to arrive in the activity room because I have to stop to wash my hands. I can feel everybody's eyeballs on me, even the half-drawn Mother Goose on the blank wall. She's giving me a look that says, You Aren't Going to Leave Me This Way, Are You?

Mr. Rodriguez says, "Good news, people. We're going to be in the newspaper."

"We are?" says Patsy Cline.

He nods and explains that he's been talking to a reporter from *The Portwaller Tribune,* who is going to come by and interview us in the next week or so and take pictures of the mural. "A headline like 'Art

Brings Kids of All Ages Together.' Or something like that. Pretty righteous, huh?"

Everybody agrees that, yes indeedy, it is very righteous.

"So," he says, "you all have a lot of work to do, like fast. What have you decided about the mural?" Mr. Rodriguez is looking at me when he asks this. And so is everybody else. "Penelope?"

"Um," I say, because when you don't know what to say, "um" does a pretty good job.

"Did you decide what you're going to put in it?" he asks.

"No, we're still waiting for *her*," says Marcus, scrunching up his face at me. "And I still think Mother Goose could live on another planet."

"Yeah," says Alexander. "She could still fly here. She's got wings, you know. Besides, they're nursery rhymes. She should be able have a laser gun to blast meteors and stuff."

If Mister Leonardo was here, he would surely say, "Now, it is one thing to have a mural that older ladies and gentlemen can enjoy while frolicking with the whippoorwills, but it is another thing entirely when all of the town will witness it in the papers. Little darling, it is your responsibility to save the mural from disastrous intentions. You know what you have to do."

Between Nila Wister, Half-Faced Mother Goose, and a dead famous artist telling me what to do, I wonder if I know how to be any sort of boss at all. Vera Bogg must be wondering the same thing, because she says, "Do you think we should vote for a new leader?"

Mr. Rodriguez frowns and puts his hand on my shoulder. "Penelope, do you want to come up with another plan?"

"*I* do," says Vera Bogg, before I have a chance to say anything.

"Me too," says Marcus.

Good gravy. I look at my half drawing of Mother Goose on the wall. I can almost hear her squawk, "Hear now, my sweet, I dare you to really take charge. And if you let them put me on an asteroid, I will lose all my feathers and promise never to forgive you."

I straighten my back a little. "I don't think Mother

Goose would want to be in outer space or driving a truck," I say. "For one thing."

"How do you know?" asks Marcus.

"Yeah," says Alexander, "did you talk to her or something?"

They laugh, Marcus and Alexander do, and Birgit joins along.

I pretend to laugh, too. I'm an excellent pretender. "Oh no," I say. "I never have. Not even one time." Because when you're the Boss, it's not a good idea for other people to know that you might sometimes talk to a half-drawn old bird.

"Maybe I could be in charge," Vera Bogg says to Mr. Rodriguez. "If Penelope doesn't want to do it."

I look at Mr. Rodriguez and he is raising his eyebrows at me like he might be thinking it's an okay idea. But it's very much not an okay idea, not to me. Because if Vera Bogg is in charge, she will become Mr. Rodriguez's Favorite. She will, I just know it. And it's not fair if she does, on account of the fact that she is already the Favorite of Miss Stunkel and Patsy Cline.

So I say no. And I say it kind of loud while I point my eyeballs in Vera's direction. Then I open up my drawing pad and hold up my sketches. "This. We're going to do this. No monster trucks, no space stations, no fleas, and most importantly, NO PINK!"

My words are heavy and thick, and they hang in the room for an awful long time. And while they do, I pretend that I don't see the wide eyes, that I don't see Patsy Cline wince when I say "flea," and that I don't see Mr. Rodriguez give me a look that says, Maybe This Isn't So Righteous.

But it's too late to go back and say never mind, so I keep going. Because when you can't go back, the only thing you can do is go frontways. I hand out my sketches and point to the blank wall. "Go," I say. "This is what we're drawing."

Somehow it works. Because the next thing I know, they've all got pencils in their drawing hands pressed up against the wall. Art is happening, my art. And everything would be all right, it would, if I didn't know the Bad Luck was somewhere lurking around a corner.

# 9.

Miss Stunkel tells us we're going to watch a short video on watercolors. "But before we do," she says, "let's hear a report on how the mural is going at Portwaller's Blessed Home for the Aging." Then she looks right at Vera Bogg, Miss Stunkel does, because I guess she doesn't know I've been voted the Boss. "Vera?" she says.

Right away Vera Bogg says, "Oh, it's going fine, I guess. Mr. Rodriguez isn't really telling us what to do much. He wants us kids to work as a group." She looks over at me when she says this last part.

"Isn't that something," says Miss Stunkel, rubbing her Monday lizard pin.

"But we needed somebody to be the decider since we only have two more weekends to work on the mural," Vera says. "So we voted, um, for a person, one of us, to be a decider. And um, um, so that's how it's going."

My word.

"Very nice," says Miss Stunkel with a smile in Vera's direction. Then she turns to the TV to start the video and I'm left out of the whole thing.

"I'm the decider," I announce. "Everyone voted for me to be the Boss of the mural. I decide."

Even Angus Meeker, who is back from the stomach bug but still looking a little gray in the face, raises his eyebrows at me.

Miss Stunkel turns around and says, "Really?" like she's surprised I'm the Boss and not Vera Bogg, who wears pink and never forgets to raise her hand before speaking and has a last name that could be Boss if the g's one day got together and decided to try something new. Then she looks at Vera like she wants to know if it's true. If I, Penelope Crumb, really am in charge. Vera's cheeks turn pinker and she nods.

So there.

Then Miss Stunkel turns back to the TV again, but before she does, she tells me I should have raised my hand before I said what I said. Not "Way to go, Penelope" or "Congratulations on your super fine achievement." But "Raise your hand before you talk. You know the rule." I tell her sorry, but I have more to say, so I raise my hand and just keep going. "We're going to be interviewed by a reporter from *The Portwaller Tribune*. So, we're going to be in the newspaper."

"That's something," says Miss Stunkel, adjusting the buttons on the TV. But she doesn't say that *I'm* something like Vera Bogg. "Thank you, Penelope. Now, let's turn our attention to the TV screen."

"The mural is about Mother Goose," I say. "Who is an actual goose that wears eyeglasses and mittens. Vera forgot to say that part."

When Miss Stunkel turns around this time, she's

got a look on her face that says, How Would You Like to Keep Talking After School? Then she says, "Which reminds me, Penelope. See me after school."

Well then.

Patsy Cline hardly talks to me all day. Even though we're not best friends anymore, and I'm the Boss and not her, it's still a good idea to talk to people once in a while. This is what I tell her as she packs up her books to go home.

Her mouth presses into a straight line, and she says, "That's mighty good advice. You should remember that yourself sometime."

Honest to goodness, that's what she says. I tell her I will try but I have a lot of things to remember these days seeing how I am the Boss and everything. Plus there's remembering to watch out for the Bad Luck, but I don't get to tell her that because by the time I think of it she's heading out the door.

Miss Stunkel must be having trouble remembering things, too, because when she calls me over to her desk, she says, "Penelope, on Friday I sent a note home with you."

This is something I'd like to forget. But what would be even better is if Miss Stunkel would forget, too. I do my best to help that along. "I don't think so," I say, shaking my head. "Nope, you didn't. Must have been someone else."

"That wasn't a question," she says, leaning in a little closer to me. "I did indeed send a note home with you on Friday."

"Oh." I eye her finger, the one that looks like a chicken bone, but she's got it tucked under a book called *The Wicked Ways of Fourth-Grade Teachers: A How-To Guide*. I'm pretty sure.

"Did the note make it to your mother?" Miss Stunkel asks.

"She's very busy." Which isn't a lie.

"So you gave her the note?"

"She has a job *and* she goes to school," I say, and then I explain how she's an insides artist and is drawing pictures of people's brains and internal organs for a book. "It's very important to get people's insides looking right."

"If she has read the note, she will know that I

asked her to sign it and for you to return it to me today."

"Doctors read those books," I say, "and you wouldn't want a doctor to mix up a brain with the thing that looks like sausage links all piled together."

"Intestine?"

"Right, intestine."

Miss Stunkel's finger twitches. "Is the note in her possession or not?"

"Not yet."

"I would like you to give it to her and then bring it back to me tomorrow," she says. "And maybe I will just give her a phone call to catch her up on things."

Just then, from somewhere around a corner, I'm pretty sure, I smell fried onions.

# 10.

ittie watches me dig into the Heap. "What are you looking for?"

At the bottom of the pile, I find my sneakers with the hole in the heel, the ones with my drawings of a big fish eating a little fish eating a worm on a hook on the sole. I toss them out. And shove my T-shirts off to the side. "A note."

"What kind of note?"

"The one from Miss Stunkel."

"Oh, Penelope."

I tell her to stop being a monkey scientist for a minute and help me look.

She tells me she will if I stop being so bossy about everything.

"But that's how I'm supposed to be," I tell her. "Because I. Am. The. Boss."

Then Littie Maple says with her hands on her hips, "Not of me, you're not."

"Don't help me look then," I say. "Fine." But then I hear the door to our apartment open and close, and so I peek out of my room and hold my breath. It's just Terrible, thank lucky stars.

Littie's eyes perk right up and she's ready with her notebook and pen. I dive back into the Heap and am buried somewhere in the middle part when I think I hear the phone ring. "Did you hear that?" I say, scrambling to the top. I pull a T-shirt off my head.

"You mean besides the phone ringing?"

"I got it!" I holler as I jump out of the Heap and race down the hall to the kitchen. Two rings, three rings, four. "I got it! I got it! I got it!" I'm almost there when from out of nowhere, Terrible picks up the phone and sticks his arm out to block me. Aliens are sneaky and fast. And sneaky.

"Hello?" he says, keeping me away with his elbow. I swipe at him, but he's covered in football padding, so nothing gets through. Then he turns his back on me and says something into the phone so quiet that I can't hear.

"Who is it?" I whisper. "Is it Miss Stunkel?"

He bats his hand at me and says a lot of "ah-huhs" and "okays." And then he's off down the hall toward the laundry room. I follow close behind, trying to listen, but I can't hear anything. "Who is it?" I ask again.

He turns around and covers the phone with his hand. He's got a look in his alien eyes that says, Stand By for Laser Beams, so I back up. And I knock right into Littie, who is behind me scribbling on her notepad.

"Go away," he whispers at us. "Now." And I think he means it.

"Just tell me if it's Miss Stunkel," I say.

Then his mouth gets so straight and thin that his lips disappear all together.

"I don't think it's Miss Stunkel," says Littie,

pulling at the back of my shirt. Then she whispers in my ear, "I think it's that *girl*."

Terrible's face turns red and he takes the phone into his room and closes the door.

"I don't like her," I say.

Littie is still writing like a mad scientist. "Who?"

"That Tildy girl. She calls all the time."

"She seemed nice enough to me," says Littie.

"What do you think she wants with my brother?"

"She must like him, I guess," she says.

"Why?"

Littie shrugs. "Probably because *he* likes *her*."

And that makes me wonder: How did Terrible get to be somebody's Favorite?

"Littie Maple," I say, "don't you ever say that."

She stops her scribbling and looks at me. "What?"

"He just doesn't, okay?" Because there isn't room for any more Favorites around here. There just isn't.

Littie stares at me for a long time and then writes something in her notebook. But when I ask what she wrote, she changes the subject and says, "Aren't you supposed to be looking for your note?"

I shake my head. "No, Littie. Forget the note. We need to find me a charm."

I lead Littie down the steps of our building to the street.

"Where are we going?" she says.

"To find a charm. Haven't you been paying attention?"

Littie tells me there I go being bossy again. Then she asks, "What kind of charm?"

"The kind that will get rid of the Bad Luck." Then I tell her about Nila Wister's charms like her butterfly and keys.

"Who's Nila Wister?" says Littie.

"Never mind," I say. "Let's just go."

Littie says she'll come but she has to be back in time for supper because her mom is fixing turkey pot pie. I tell her fine but I don't know how she can think about food when the Bad Luck is all around, and then we head down the street.

I keep my eyeballs on the sidewalk and the storefront windows, watching for I-don't-know-what to say "Here I am, little darling, the charm you've been looking for, the one that will make all your troubles go away."

After three blocks, I don't see any. And I know the Bad Luck is to blame.

Littie says, "If a good-luck charm can be a butterfly figurine or some keys, then it could be anything, right?"

"Right."

"Then how do we know what we're looking for?" she says. "I mean, couldn't that tree over there be a good-luck charm?"

I tell her that I'll know a charm when I see it, at least I think I will, and that a tree can't be a good-luck charm because everybody knows that a good-luck charm has to fit in your pocket. My word.

As we're walking along in the next block, a commuter bus speeds by, and the wind blows my ponytail the whole way around my head, tickling my nose. A sign hanging from a nearby storefront swings and creaks. It reads ROCK OF AGES, and in the front window are baskets of colored stones and crystals. "Let's go in here."

Inside, the store stinks. Not like fried onions, thank lucky stars, but like heavy perfume on dusty curtains. And it makes my nose burn. "Looking for something?" says a man behind the counter. He has a big nose, like a flower bulb, and I wonder how he can stand the smell of this place. When I ask him, he says, "I don't know what you mean."

I give him a look that says, You Should Be Able to Smell Roses on the Moon, but if he doesn't know he has a big nose in the middle of his face, then I'm not going to be the one to tell him.

"We're looking for good-luck charms," says Littie.

"You don't say," says the man.

I tell him that we do say and ask if there are any in the store. He says that he can't guarantee any luck with a purchase but that we're welcome to look around and see if anything strikes us as lucky. And also, all sales are final.

"If something strikes us," I whisper to Littie, "I don't think we'd be very lucky."

She rolls her eyes at me and then we start looking. After a few minutes of it, I decide that rocks aren't very exciting. And they don't feel very lucky. Littie asks about a shiny rock in the display case, for who knows why, and the man tells her that it is quartz crystal. From the mountains just north of Portwaller.

When Littie asks whether it's rose quartz or smoky quartz, I say, "Are these supposed to be good luck or something?"

Littie says, no, but aren't they pretty?

"Littie Maple," I say, "if you have to get home for turkey pot pie, I don't think we have time to look at rocks that don't do anything but sit there and look pretty."

The man tells Littie they are rose quartz in case she still wants to know, and then after he puts them back into the display case, he points to Littie's cheek and tells her she's got an eyelash there. She brushes off her cheek with her fingers, and the man says, "Oh, you should have made a wish."

"What?" asks Littie.

"You put your eyelash here," he says, pointing to the top of his fist, "and then blow it off and make a wish. Haven't you heard of that before?"

I look at Littie and we both shake our heads. "So an eyelash is kind of like a good-luck charm?" I say.

"No," says the man. "I wouldn't say that."

"But you can make a wish with it," I say.

He says, yeah, you can.

"Then it's a good-luck charm."

"No, not really."

"But it is."

"I don't think so."

"Then what is it?" I ask.

"Um . . ."

"See, if you don't know, then it must be a charm."

He shakes his head. "That's not . . ."

"It is, I'm sure of it."

"No."

"It has to be." And before he has a chance to tell me different, I grab Littie.

"Thank you," says Littie as I pull her out the door. "Very pretty quartz!"

Out on the sidewalk I tell Littie to check my face for fallen eyelashes.

"What?" she says.

"Do you know how many wishes I've missed out on? Come on, I don't want to miss out on any more."

She looks real close. So close I can tell she ate an orange some time ago and also peanut butter. "I don't see any. Try blinking hard. Maybe one will fall out."

I open and shut my eyes as fast as I can, and the lights go on and then off and then on and then off and then on and then I hold on to Littie's shoulder because I start to feel dizzy.

Littie shakes her head. "Nothing."

"They must be in there good," I say.

She tells me to try rubbing my eyes. "That might knock one loose."

I do. For a long time, until everything is a little blurry. "How about now?"

"Nope."

I sigh. "Well then, you'll have to get one."

"What do you mean, *get one*?"

"You know, yank one out," I say. "It's the only way."

"Are you sure?" asks Littie.

I nod.

Littie brings her fingers close to my eyeball and I go all stiff. "You're not going to get mad at me if it hurts, are you?" she says

"No," I say. "I promise. Just try not to make it hurt."

Littie moves her fingers closer, so close it looks like a giant pterodactyl coming in to pluck out my eyeball. Then it flies away. "You sure you're not going to get mad?"

"Littie Maple, I already said I promise."

"It's getting dark out here, so it's getting hard to see," she says.

"Then you better hurry."

She tells me that I better stop being so bossy and that she's just trying to help. I tell her less trying more doing, and that's when the pterodactyl returns and grabs at my eyeball.

"Yeeoow!"

"Did you get one?"

Littie says no and then makes another grab without warning.

"Oow oww!" I cover my eye with my hand.

She examines her fingers and holds her hand up in the air. "I got it!"

With one good eye, I give her a look that says, Littie Maple Saves the Day. I put out my fist to her. "Put it here. Put it here."

Littie's tongue is wagging sideways out of her mouth as she puts the eyelash on my hand. She puts it there real slow, and I think it will never get there and I'll never get to make my wish, but then it does get there, my eyelash does. And it's a real beauty.

Littie says, "There. Make your wish for good luck."

And just as I'm about to, wouldn't you know the Bad Luck sends another bus speeding by, blowing my eyelash to who knows where, and taking my wish right along with it.

# 11.

Here's one thing I know about trouble: It's really good at following you places. I know this because as soon as I get home, my mom yells from the laundry room, "If that's you, Penelope, we have some talking to do!"

Good gravy.

I say, "It's not Penelope. It's someone else. Someone who doesn't need to talk about anything unless it has to do with getting more sweets in the cupboards. But thanks very much, anyway, I'll be across the hall eating some turkey pot pie." I say this in a tiny voice, in barely a whisper, with cupped hands over my mouth. If Mom doesn't know it's me that's just come inside, then I'm not going to be the one to tell her.

I tiptoe backwards toward the door, but then I see Terrible's head poking out from the kitchen. He's biting an orange Popsicle in half.

"Ah! Where did you get that?" I say.

"The freezer."

"Save me an orange one," I say.

He says, "Save me from having to look at you."

Aliens. I try to move past him, but he blocks me. I grit my teeth, but that just makes him laugh. Then I give him a sideways look that says, Does That Girl Tildy Know about Your Alien Ways?

But he doesn't have a chance to answer because Mom yells my name again. And she says it like she's talking about one of the gross insides she draws. Kidney stone, for example.

Terrible shoves the rest of the Popsicle in his mouth and then smiles so I can see all of his orange teeth.

"I'm coming," I yell.

Mom is sitting at her drawing desk. Which is really our broken dryer. She tells me to have a seat, but since it's the laundry room and there are no other chairs, I sit on the floor next to a pile of dirty socks. She piles her hair into a messy bun on the top of her head and sticks in two drawing pencils to keep it in place. "I got a phone call today," she says.

"Was it from a doctor about your brain pictures?" I say. "Because they are very good." I pick up one of her drawing pads on the floor by her stool and open it. Brains everywhere, and somebody's back, too, with all of the backbones.

"Penelope Rae." (Infected hair follicle.)

But I keep going, asking her if I have all those tiny bones in my back like her picture does and telling her that Littie's momma is going to have a baby just in case she sees her in the hall and thinks she's been eating too many pastries. Because sometimes if you just keep talking about bones and babies and fat bellies and things like that, people will forget that they are mad at you and want to send you to your room without any Popsicles.

"I want to talk about the phone call I just got from Miss Stunkel."

Sometimes this doesn't work so good.

"Is there something you want to tell me?" she asks.

"No," I say. And that's the honest truth.

"Why didn't you tell me that Miss Stunkel sent another note home?"

I tell her that I didn't want to get into trouble. But then she asks me if I don't think I'm in trouble now.

Oh.

Then she tells me no TV for a week, two extra nights of doing dishes, and I'm to come straight home from school and go to my room to do all of my homework. She says I should go ahead there now and think about how I can improve my behavior and stop from getting any more notes sent home. "Go on, now. To your room. Which by the way is still a huge mess. You need to clean it, or I will."

Having your mom clean your room sounds like it would be a good thing, but it very much is not.

That's how my Favorite T-shirt ended up in the rag bag.

Then she sets her eraser on one of her drawings and starts rubbing out the marks. She rubs so hard you can't even tell the lines were there.

I stare at her drawing and watch the lines disappear. "I don't know how I can stop getting any more notes sent home. I'm not Miss Stunkel's Favorite."

Mom looks at me like she doesn't know why I'm still standing here talking about Miss Stunkel after she told me to go to my room. "I don't think you need to be her Favorite to behave in her class," she says. "I was in fourth grade, too, once."

"A very, very, long, long, long time ago," I tell her. Then I give her a look that says, Notice I Didn't Say O-L-D. "And your teacher was probably a lot nicer than Miss Stunkel."

Mom shakes her head at me and then puts down her eraser. "I don't understand, Penelope. You seem to be able to follow my rules at home. At least most of the time." And just as she says this, she gets a look on her face like she's thinking about all the times I haven't followed her rules. Which is a lot. "Well, wait . . ."

I quick change the subject. "But you like me," I say.

She nods and then her mouth curls into a smile. "I do."

"I'm your Favorite."

She stops smiling. "My what?"

"Your Favorite," I say. "You know, person."

"Oh."

That's what she says: Oh.

My toes get crampy. "Aren't I?"

She doesn't say, "Oh my darling, oh my heart. Of course you are." Instead, she pinches my cheek, smoothes my hair, and says, "Well, moms don't have Favorites. It's a rule."

I know this is what moms have to say, I know. But when it's between me and an alien, ME or an ALIEN, I'd like to think that maybe, just maybe, ME, Penelope Crumb, might win out. I give her a smile that says, It's Okay, I Won't Tell Anybody. And even if I did, nobody would blame her for not loving an alien very much, I think.

"Oh, Penelope," she says. "I love you as much as I love your brother."

Well then.

It's a long walk down the hall. I can hear Terrible talking to somebody on the phone. He's sprawled out on the couch with his stinky feet hanging off the end. I tiptoe closer, trying to be quiet like I have slippers made of cotton balls. Terrible does a lot of "ah-huhs" and "okays" and "yeahs." And I think he must be talking to that Tildy girl again. Then he says, "All right, see you on Saturday, Grandpa Felix," and hangs up.

"Grandpa Felix?" I say.

My cotton ball feet must work real good because Terrible jumps and hollers my name. I guess aliens aren't the only ones who can be sneaky.

"What?"

"Didn't Grandpa Felix want to talk to me?" I ask.

"I guess not."

This hurts like a knuckle punch in the arm. "Well, what are you doing with him on Saturday?"

"Nosy, aren't you?" he says.

I stick my big nose in the air and give him a look that says, Yes Indeedy, I Am.

"I'm helping Grandpa with a photo shoot," says Terrible, "if you need to know."

"You can't do that," I say. I'm the one that helps Grandpa with his photography jobs. That's my job. That's what I do. That's what we do together.

"Nosy *and* bossy." He shakes his head at me.

Littie pushes open the door to our apartment then. "Penelope! Oh, good, you're right here. I brought you something to make up for your eyelash problem." She shoves a folded paper towel at me.

I give Littie a look that says, Not in Front of the Alien.

But she isn't so good at telling what different faces mean. "You know," she says, "when we tried to pull one out. For luck."

"Littie Maple!"

"What?" she says.

Terrible gives us both the Hairy Eyeball and says, "You are so weird."

Littie hands me the paper towel. "Open it, and be very careful."

I unfold the paper towel and nearly go dead when I see what Littie brought me.

"It's a wishbone," says Littie, "from the turkey my mom made." She says it like I may not know what a wishbone is or that it comes from inside a turkey.

I tell her I know, I know, and this is way better than an eyelash especially because there's no pterodactyl trying to make me go blind. I take one side of the wishbone and hold it out for Littie to take the other.

Littie shakes her head. "No, not me." Then she points to Terrible. "You do it." She grabs her notebook and pen from her back pocket and she's a scientist again.

Before I can tell Littie that this is a very bad idea, Terrible is off the couch and has got his alien fingers wrapped around the other side of the wishbone.

"Wait!" I yell. "I'm not ready." I think of my wish, putting the words together in my head so that I get it right. And when I do I tell Littie to count to three.

She nods and then looks at us to see if we've got our wishes ready. Terrible smiles at me. I know that smile. It says, Losers Never Win. And that's just awful, especially after he's taking my place with Grandpa Felix, after not being Mom's Favorite, after not being anybody's Favorite, after all the Bad Luck. So awful that I definitely go dead this time. I'm sure of it, because I don't hear Littie say, "Three." But she must've, because the next thing I know, Terrible has pulled on the wishbone and my side snaps in half.

# 12.

I'm not talking to Grandpa. I'm not talking to him the whole way to Portwaller's Blessed Home for the Aging.

I just look out the car window and squeeze the paper lunch bag in my lap. The orange Popsicle inside is already starting to melt.

"Are you going to tell me what's got you miffed, or would you like me to guess?" says Grandpa Felix.

I say, "Humph," and then nothing else. If Grandpa Felix doesn't know that I'm his Favorite, and that it should always be me as his photographer's assistant, not Terrible, then I'm not going to be the one to tell him.

"Suit yourself," he says. And we go along for the rest of the drive without saying anything.

As I get out of the car, Grandpa says that Mom will be picking me up this afternoon, and not him. "I've got a wedding to photograph this afternoon," he says. "Your brother is going to help me."

"Is that so?" I say. Even though I already know it is so, I pretend that I don't, and I don't know why.

Grandpa Felix says, "I asked your brother to help me because I knew you were busy today with your mural project."

"I could have left early," I say.

He sighs. "So this is what your grump is about."

"I just wanted to be the one to help you," I say.

"There will be other shoots," he says. "And I don't spend near as much time with Terrence as I do with you."

That's because he's Terrible the Alien. But I decide to keep that to myself for now.

"I'll be by to bring you here tomorrow morning

same as usual." Then he waves at me, the kind of wave a grandpa might give to some girl who he likes okay but is certainly not his Favorite, and drives away.

Before my Popsicle puddles, I bring it to Nila Wister. The door to her room is open, so I go right on in. "I brought you some sweets today," I say. "I hope you like orange."

Nila sits in her wheelchair, facing the window. She doesn't say a word, not even "Big mistake," and I worry that she's gone dead from not enough sugary sweets. That would be just like the Bad Luck.

Slowly I walk toward her, whispering her name. Because you don't ever want to sneak up on an old person. They could go dead just from the scare. I stick out my finger and when I get close enough to touch her, I can already feel her cold Graveyard Dead skin on my fingertip. I poke her anyway, right in her cheek, and she screams, "I'm going!"

I drop my Popsicle. Because when somebody who is Graveyard Dead comes back to life, it can make you forget you've got something in your hands.

Nila Wister turns her old eyeballs on me and says, "Did you just poke me in the face?"

I nod and say, "Congratulations, you're alive!"

"Of course I'm alive," she growls. "What did you think?"

"That you weren't."

"Well, I am. At least for this moment," she says. Then she looks me over. "So, give me some candies."

I pick up the Popsicle and hand it to her. She gives it a squeeze. "A little squishy, isn't it?"

I tell her sorry about the melting.

She turns it over in her hands. "What flavor?"

"Orange."

She nods. "My Favorite."

I smile and tell her I have to work on the mural now but will stop by after. "I need to ask you about the trouble. It hasn't gone away."

Nila Wister nods and says, "I know. And there's something I need to ask you."

"What?"

"Just go on now," she says. "Let me drink my Popsicle in peace."

Mr. Rodriguez looks a little worried. Patsy Cline, Vera, and Marcus are huddled around him, and they all have looks on their faces that say, This Is Very Not Good. They all look at me when I come into the activity room, but only for a second.

"Penelope," says Mr. Rodriguez, "we were just going over the game plan."

"Oh," I say, and drag a chair over to the table beside Patsy Cline. Because I should know the game plan, too, seeing how I'm the Boss and everything.

"Birgit is sick," says Mr. Rodriguez, "so she's not coming today."

I look around at the others and notice that Alexander isn't here either. "I hope it's not the stomach bug."

Patsy Cline groans just then. And I can tell she's worried that she's going to get the stomach bug, too, because she asks if maybe one of the nurses has masks we could all wear to keep out the germs. "And some hand sanitizer," she says. "I can make a list."

"Poor Birgit," says Vera Bogg.

"And Alexander," I say, nodding.

Then Mr. Rodriguez says, "Well, Alexander isn't sick." He clears his throat. "He's had a change of heart about the mural and decided to spend his weekends doing something else."

Marcus says, "Humph," and then nothing else. And he's looking at me when he says it.

Mr. Rodriguez pats Marcus on the shoulder and says, "That's enough talk out of me. You guys have a lot of work to do. So I'll let you get to it."

I pull my No. 2 Hard drawing pencil from my pocket and go to the wall. I'm working on the cuffs of Mother Goose's woolen mittens when I notice that nobody else is drawing. Patsy Cline is chewing on an eraser. Vera Bogg is playing with the flower on her headband. And Marcus is giving me the Stink Eye.

If Mister Leonardo was here, he'd surely say, "What trouble is plaguing these souls that their hands cannot grip a pencil?"

I give them all a look that says, Start Drawing, Pronto. And then I say, "Start drawing, pronto." I think it's really too bad that I don't have anything

like Miss Stunkel's chicken-bone finger because it might come in handy at a time like this.

Even without Miss Stunkel's finger, Patsy Cline, Vera Bogg, and Marcus start to draw, thank lucky stars. A billion years later. And when they do, I only have to tell them a couple of times to redo what they've done.

"Jack Be Nimble looks more like a Janet," I tell Vera Bogg.

I say to Marcus, "The moon has too many craters."

"Pussycat's whiskers are too thick," I tell Patsy Cline. "He'd never be able to lift his head off the ground."

By the end of the day, I'm really tired. Being in charge is hard work. When I say, "See you to-morrow," to everybody, only Patsy Cline answers. "You're being a bit too bossy," she says up close and in a whisper. "More than a bit, if you want to know the truth."

"What do you mean?"

"The way you tell us all what to do all the time," she says.

"Patsy Cline," I say, "this is what bosses are supposed to do."

She shakes her head at me.

"Have you ever been a Boss?" I ask.

"No, and neither have you been until now, I believe. But I don't have to be one to know what bossy looks like. And it looks a lot like you, Penelope Crumb."

"I told you that I liked the Pussycat's whiskers, didn't I?" I say. "After the last time you redrew them."

"The only reason I drew them so big in the first place was because I got a little spooked when I saw his tail." Patsy Cline folds her arms across her chest. "And, no, you did not tell me that even once."

"Well, I meant to."

"But you didn't." Patsy Cline stares at me, I don't know what for, and when I tell her I have to go meet somebody, she looks like she's just seen another tail and is about to have an allergic reaction. Then she says, "Well, I guess if you have to go."

I've only got a couple of minutes before Mom will

be here to pick me up, so I wave at Patsy Cline and walk as fast as I can to find Nila Wister. She's just where I left her this morning, staring out the same window. I go in without knocking and sit down beside her wheelchair. "I did it," I tell her. "I stood up to the trouble, but it's still hanging around."

Nila keeps her eyes on whatever is happening outside her window. This time I don't poke her cheek, I poke her hands, which are folded together in her lap.

"Nila?"

"That was a good Popsicle," she tells me. "Got any more?"

I say there's more at home unless the alien ate them all. Then I ask, "Did you hear what I said? The trouble is still here. Now what?"

She unfolds her hands. Inside them is the butterfly figurine that had been hanging from her wheelchair. "You want my help?" she whispers.

I nod.

"Then I need *your* help."

"For what?" I say, because if this is about more

Popsicles, between Nila Wister and Terrible, I'll never be able to have any for myself ever.

She tells me to come closer. I get up on my knees and lean in so that I've got a pretty good view of the butterfly, and I bring my finger toward it. Because maybe if I can just touch it once, just once, I can have some of its good luck for myself. But before my finger gets too close, Nila closes up her hands. Then her tiny voice comes out in a whisper. "I have to go."

I whisper back, "Okay, do you want me to get the nurse?" Because I don't know anything about helping an old lady go to the bathroom, and I don't want to.

Nila Wister rolls her eyeballs at me and shakes her head. "Not that, foolish girl," she says. "I want to leave this place."

"You do?"

"And if you help me," she says, lifting the butterfly charm in her hands, "I'll help you."

# 13.

The alien is stealing Grandpa Felix. I know this because at dinner, Grandpa Felix is going on and on about how Terrible did so good at helping him with the wedding shoot. And how Terrible is the greatest photographer's assistant in the whole wide world. And that if he knew how amazing and spectacular Terrible was, he wouldn't have been spending so much time with me.

Okay, so maybe he didn't say that last part exactly, or the first, truth be told, but it's what he meant. I'm pretty sure.

Our kitchen table is extra crowded because Tildy

the girl is having dinner with us, too. She smiles a lot, mostly at Terrible, and so does Mom. And all of a sudden, I wonder if I somehow went dead for real because nobody seems to notice that I'm here.

"Can I have some more bread?" I say. Not because I want any. I've got a whole buttered slice on my plate right next to my spaghetti and meatballs. But because I want to see if I'm really dead or not.

I must be, because nobody gives me any. And nobody says, "Of course, Penelope, have all the bread you want." They just keep on talking about things that don't have anything to do with me and that have everything to do with the alien.

I can almost hear the meatballs say, "We've been sitting on her plate forever and nobody has even noticed the girl's not eating. Maybe we should get somebody's attention."

Next to me, Grandpa Felix cuts his meatball with his fork just then, and half of it rolls off his plate and onto my lap. "Oh, dear," he says, "My meatball seems to have grown legs."

Terrible laughs like this is the funniest thing he's

ever heard. He smiles at Grandpa and at Tildy the girl. He looks so happy, Terrible does, like he's never even heard of the Bad Luck. And this makes my face hot.

Grandpa doesn't even notice that I haven't picked up the meatball off my lap. And Mom doesn't say anything about the tomato sauce and meat stain on my pants. It's in the shape of a stomach ulcer. Which won't come out in the wash.

Then Grandpa tells a story about something that happened at the photography shoot today, something that Terrible did that made his job a whole lot easier and helped him get some of the best wedding pictures he's taken in a long time. That's what he says while I, Penelope Crumb, his regular photographer's assistant and used-to-be Favorite, sit here with half a ball of meat in my lap.

Then Tildy the girl speaks. "I had no idea you were such a good photographer," she tells Terrible.

"He's not," I say, finally getting alive again. Everybody looks at me now that I've come back from the dead and have something to say.

Mom says, "Penelope Rae." (Gingivitis.)

"He's the assistant, truth be told," I say. "And the assistant doesn't get to take pictures. Right, Grandpa Felix?"

But instead of saying, "Right you are, little darling. And if I let anyone take pictures it would be you because you've been asking forever and also because I love you the most," instead of that he says, "Well . . ." and sort of shrugs. His face turns Vera Bogg pink.

"Right, Grandpa?" I say again. Because he's old and sometimes you have to say things twice.

"Um," he says.

"You let HIM take pictures but you won't let me!" I yell. I'm up on my feet, and the meatball slides down my leg to the floor.

Mom calls my name again and says for goodness' sakes hold it together. Grandpa Felix tells me not to make a big deal out of this, that it just worked out that Terrible was in a better position for the shot. Only he doesn't say *Terrible*, he says *Terrence*, and that's when I decide to announce to everyone, including the girl Tildy, that my brother, who they all know as Terrence, is really, honest to goodness, an alien. The kind from outer space. And who is all of a sudden trying to fool everyone into thinking he's not by playing football and talking to girls.

Terrible spits his spaghetti into his napkin, because now the truth is out and the last thing he'd want is a mouthful of spaghetti when NASA scientists knock on our door.

But then the Bad Luck squeezes.

Mom's face gets all blotchy, and at first I think it's because she has an alien for a son. Whose face wouldn't get blotchy at news like that? But then she gives me a look that says, Not Another Word, Missy. And even though I can tell she really wants to, Mom doesn't say anything. Probably because Tildy the girl is sitting right there, and it's not a good idea to holler at the dinner table in front of a guest. Mom likes guests to think that we're a normal, non-hollering type of family, I suppose.

I'm about to explain how I know Terrible is an alien, that there's proof if they would just listen, but

Grandpa Felix squeezes my shoulder, kind of hard, too, and I close my mouth. Then he asks Tildy the girl about her favorite subject in school. And just like that, everybody pretends I'm not here, that Terrible's not from another planet, and that I haven't been meatballed for no reason.

Later, Littie Maple knocks on my door. "Do sisters have to share everything?" she wants to know.

I say, "Absolutely positively no. And it's better if you put your name on everything that's yours including Popsicles, because once that baby has teeth, and maybe even before, nothing will be just yours."

"Oh," says Littie, writing that down.

Then I open the drawer to my desk and pull out the colors I got from May's Hardware. "Here," I say, handing them over to Littie, "I got you Celery Stalk, Morning Dewdrop, and my favorite, Rustic Forest."

"Rustic Forest?" she says.

"I decided the new baby's room should be green."

"You did?"

I nod. "When are you going to start painting? Because I can help with that, too."

Littie looks at her feet. "Sorry, Penelope," she says. "Momma and I already picked out the color."

"Without me?"

Littie says yes.

I fold my arms across my chest and wait for Littie to tell me.

"Yellow," she says.

"Yellow?" I say. "What kind of yellow? Morning Sunrise? Canary Feather? Citrus Lemon?"

"I don't know," she says. "Just yellow."

I shake my head and say to Littie what Nila Wister is always saying to me: "Big mistake."

She says, "What's wrong with yellow?"

"Not a thing," I say. Because if Littie wants the new baby to feel like it's about to be run over by a school bus, then I'm not going to be the one to tell her different.

"Let's not have a fight," she tells me.

"Oh, you'll need to get used to that," I say, "because having a brother or sister means fights, lots of them. Sometimes over the stuff that's not yours anymore and sometimes just because. You could be walking down the hall and from out of nowhere your brother or sister just jumps out at you and pushes you for no reason."

"Really?"

I tell her, yes, really.

She writes that down, too, and then says, "What else?"

"You really want to know?" I say.

She nods, but I'm not so sure she does. Either way, I let her have it with the truth. "When you're a sister, you have to put up with the stink of another person in the family. And you better hope it's not a boy, because they smell the worst. And if for some reason your brother or sister gets snatched by aliens and returned like my brother was, you are in for a world of trouble, not to mention the worst kind of stink ever."

Littie stops writing, but she's still listening, so I keep going. "Right now, you are your momma's and dad's All-Time Favorite. Your grandma's and grandpa's Favorite, too. Only you won't be for long. And even if you ever do get to be again, sometime in the future, your brother or sister will do something, like take a dumb picture, that everybody will think is very much wonderful enough to be in a museum or something, and then you will die right in front of them, and nobody will notice. And they will throw hamburger at you. And think it's funny. Because you are just the used-to-be Favorite and who cares about that?"

Littie Maple looks like she might cry.

I tell her that I'm sorry but she wanted to know the truth.

She closes up her notebook and slides her pen through the spiral rings. "Maybe that's just how it is over here," she says. "That doesn't mean that's how it's going to be for me."

I shrug.

Then she tells me, "Jane Goodall was lucky the chimps couldn't tell her these kinds of things!"

"Don't get sore at me," I say. "I was just trying to help."

But all she says is "humph" and nothing else and then slams the door on her way out.

# 14.

Except to tell me that he's very disappointed in the way I behaved last night at dinner, Grandpa Felix is quiet the whole way to the nursing home. Which suits me fine, because if he doesn't know that I'm still mad at him for letting an alien take pictures when he never lets me, then I'm not going to be the one to tell him.

If you ask me, he doesn't have any reason to be mad at me. After all, he wasn't the one with a meatball in his lap.

I don't have a Popsicle for Nila, and I don't have an answer for her either. So I go straight to the activity room. When I get there, I know something is wrong. Besides the half-drawn mural, it's just Patsy Cline and Mr. Rodriguez. "Where is everybody?"

Patsy Cline gives me a look that says, You Don't Want to Know.

"Have a seat," says Mr. Rodriguez.

I can almost hear Mother Goose ruffle her feathers and say, "It really is a shame that this is turning out to be quite a mess. Oh dear."

Mr. Rodriguez scratches his chin beard. "Penelope, they aren't coming. The others, they want to quit."

"How come?" Then I look at Patsy Cline. "Even Vera Bogg?"

She shrugs, and then nods.

Mr. Rodriguez says that he's sorry and that it's his fault really. That I shouldn't take it personally.

"Why would I do that?" I say.

Patsy Cline looks me straight in the face and says everybody skedaddled because of me being so bossy and, for crying out loud, people can only take so much. And that's just how she says it.

Mr. Rodriguez pats me on the back and says that

he should have been more hands-on from the beginning and that he only wanted us to learn to work as a team, so that the mural was one hundred percent ours, but that didn't happen. "And now . . ."

"But Patsy Cline and me are here," I say.

His shoulders slump. "The party for the unveiling of the mural is next Saturday. Which means we've got today and a few hours on Saturday morning to finish up." He points to the wall. "The drawing isn't finished, and you haven't even started painting. I just don't think the two of you will be able to finish in time. I'm sorry."

"What if we worked on it in the evenings, after school?" I say, pretending that Mom would let me do that even after she told me I should come straight home.

He says that won't work because the old people use the activity room on weeknights. Then he says, "Penelope, I'm sorry, but I'm going to take over. I've got to see if I can get the others to come back and help. And while I'm doing that, you two can start painting."

"But we aren't finished the drawings yet," I say. The pufferbellies have different-size wheels, the Man on the Moon looks like he's got the measles, the cat from Hey Diddle Diddle needs a fiddle and not something that is supposed to be a fiddle but looks like a guitar, and Hickory Dickory looks more like a sausage than a clock. Mister Leonardo would say, "Unsatisfactory, if you ask me."

"We're going with what we have," he says. "We have to. Otherwise on Saturday there will be nothing at all to celebrate."

Oh.

Mr. Rodriguez pulls his cell phone from his pocket and tells us he'll be back. "Wish me luck," he says.

Patsy Cline tells him good luck, but I don't say anything because what's the point? The Good Luck wouldn't listen to me anyway.

When he's gone, Patsy Cline asks me if she should keep working on Pussycat's whiskers. I tell her I'm not the Boss anymore, so do what you want. She says, "Don't be like that, now." Then she goes over to the wall and starts drawing.

While Patsy Cline draws, she sings real softly, *"If I could see the world / through the eyes of a child / smiling faces would greet me all the while / like a lovely work of art / it would warm my weary heart / just to see through the eyes of a child."*

And I don't know if it's Patsy Cline's sweet voice or my own weary heart, or maybe both, but I say all at once, "I just wanted you to like me again."

She turns away from the mural to look at me. "I like you fine."

"Not more than Vera Bogg," I whisper.

Patsy Cline doesn't say anything. Because either she doesn't hear me or she does and there's nothing much else to say.

"How come you came back?" I ask.

She shrugs. "Singing is just me, by myself. And I wanted to do something with people. I'm not like you, I'm not real good at drawing, but it makes me feel nice. And maybe, when we're all done, other people will feel nice, too."

That's when I know that this whole time, being the Boss, I haven't felt so nice. And that maybe the mural shouldn't be so much about me trying to be a famous artist. That maybe the mural shouldn't be *about* anything at all, but instead should be *for* something. I tell this to Patsy Cline and she says, "I'm sure I don't know what you mean."

I say never mind and then say, "I'm glad you came back, Patsy Cline."

She gives me a smile that says, I Never Really Left.

And when somebody gives you a present like that, it's only right to give them one back. So I climb onto a chair and take my No. 2 Hard drawing pencil out of my pocket. Up high, above the moon, I draw a cow, one with hearts instead of spots.

Patsy Cline's smile is so big her cheeks have nearly disappeared.

I tell her I'm sorry about not voting for her to be the Boss and for thinking her drawing was a flea even after she told me it wasn't, twice, and she says that's okay.

"If you were the Boss," I say, "everybody would probably still be here."

"Probably so," she says.

"But if you were the Boss," I say, "the mural would also look like a bunch of fleas."

Patsy Cline giggles. Which makes me laugh, and for a second I forget about Nila Wister's escape and about the Bad Luck that might never go away. Because when you make your used-to-be best friend giggle like that, all you want to do is make her giggle again.

I try to think of something else funny to say, but I can't think for very long because Mr. Rodriguez and another man come into the room. Mr. Rodriguez says that this man is from *The Portwaller Tribune* and then he tells him our names.

"Is this the mural?" the man says, moving closer to the wall to have a look.

Mr. Rodriguez says that it is, and the reporter says he thought it would be more complete than this. "I've got a photographer on the way, and these drawings aren't going to show up in a photograph too well," he says, shaking his head.

"We're going to start painting today," I say. "Maybe your photographer can come back later to take some pictures? Maybe on Saturday, when we're all done?"

"That's not going to work," he says. "This was the only window she has available. A lot of our staff have been out sick with a stomach bug."

Then I say, "My grandpa is a photographer, and he's taken pictures for your newspaper before. He's coming on Saturday, if he can stand the smell."

Mr. Rodriguez gives us a look that says, You Two Should Get Back to Drawing. So, I pull on Patsy Cline's arm and lead her back to the wall. I pick up my No. 2 Hard drawing pencil and pretend to work on the Man on the Moon's nose. But what I'm really doing is listening and sneaking looks.

Mr. Rodriguez tells the reporter about how he wanted the mural to be as much for the kids as the old people, only he doesn't say old people, he says residents.

"Are these two girls the only ones working on this?" asks the reporter. "I thought there'd be a bigger group."

Mr. Rodriguez scratches his chin beard and then

says in a low voice, but not too low that I can't hear, "Well, we've had some artistic, er . . . pains, you know, getting everyone on the same page."

"What sorts of pains?" asks the reporter, taking out a notepad and pen from his pocket.

Mr. Rodriguez gives me a sideways look real fast, and I wince and look away.

"He means me," I whisper to Patsy Cline. "I am an Artistic Pain."

"I know," she says.

I put down my No. 2 Hard drawing pencil and stop listening to what Mr. Rodriguez is saying. I look at the mural, at all the work that needs to be done, and my ears start to sweat. "What if the others don't come back?"

Patsy Cline shakes her head. "I don't think just you and me can do this by Saturday."

"I don't think so either." And I know it's my fault.

"We just need some luck, that's all," says Patsy Cline, and she says it real simple, as if you can just reach up and pull some from a bookshelf, or from a tree.

Or from a Fortune Lady.

# 15.

When Nila Wister sees me and my empty hands, she says, "Big mistake."

I tell her I'm sorry but we're down to one Popsicle in the freezer at home and it's been a rough week.

"Humph," she says, and nothing else, like she knows all about rough weeks. And I guess if you are as ancient as Nila Wister, you've probably had a lot of those.

I stare at her for a while, a long while, and then I say, "If I help you, you'll give me one of your charms?"

She nods. "That's the arrangement."

"And the charm will work," I say, "you know, to get rid of the Bad Luck?"

"Yes, indeed."

"But you said they can be a little particular," I tell her.

Nila frowns. "That's right, I guess I did." She shifts in her chair like my questions are making her tired. "But not if you believe."

"Believe what?"

"That it will work."

"Oh." I watch the charms dangle from her chair as she leans forward, closer to me.

"So you'll help me then?" she says as one corner of her mouth curls.

"Why don't you like it here?"

Nila Wister's face falls because it's another question. "This place?" she says. "Oh, it's all right, if you like the sort of place where nobody seems to even be bothered you're here, except when they come into your room anytime they please, and tell you that you've had too many sweets. Does that sound like a place you'd want to live?"

"That sounds a lot like where I do live," I say. Because it does.

"My sister brought me a chocolate every day," she says, smiling. "She was the youngest of all of us, but I was always her Favorite."

"I'd like to be somebody's Favorite," I say softly.

But whether Nila hears me or not I don't know because then she says, "Did you know when she was a baby, I pretended that she was mine. I dressed her up in a ruffled bonnet and carried her around like she was a china doll." Nila is looking out the window when she says all this, like she's reciting a dream to herself. "I once had a sweet little doll, dears. The prettiest doll in the world. Her cheeks were so red and white, dears, and her hair was so charmingly curled. But I lost my poor little doll, dears . . ." Nila's tiny voice trails off, and when her eyes wander over to me, she gives me a look like she forgot I was here.

"What will it be?" she says.

"Where will you go?"

"Home."

"But if you want to go home, why can't you just tell the people here that you want to leave?" I say.

She shakes her head and gives me a look that says, You Don't Know Anything. And then I know it wasn't up to her to come here in the first place.

"What about the rest of your family?" I say. "Are they Graveyard Dead, too?"

"You ask a lot of questions for someone so small and unlucky," she says. "I've got a brother left, but I don't know where he is. We aren't that friendly."

"Oh."

"So, will you help me or not?" she says.

"Don't you have any kids or anything?"

"What, girl?"

"Any kids," I say.

"None."

"Is it because you don't like kids?"

She raises her eyebrows at me. "I like them all right. Some of them, anyway."

"Do you like *me* then?" I ask. Because I wonder if maybe I could be her Favorite. Seeing how it seems like we're both alone.

"You?" she says.

I nod and whisper, "Me."

"You could stand to bring me more sweets," she says. "Something other than melted Popsicles." She looks me over and shrugs. "But I guess you're okay."

"Then could I be your Favorite?" I say. "And you could be mine."

She scrunches up her lips like she's thinking hard about it. And then all at once, she shrugs her bony shoulders and says, "Deal."

"Okay," I say, "then I'll help you."

Nila Wister smacks her tiny hands on the blanket covering her lap. "Good girl. I'm liking you more already." She tells me to come closer and then whispers, "I've been doing some thinking, and the best time is right in the middle of the big party, when everyone will be in that room eyeing up your painting. You'll have to sneak away. Do you think you can do that?"

"This Saturday?" I say. "That's awful soon."

"I'm ninety-three," she yells. "Wait much longer and the next chance I have to go home is in a pine box. Do you think you can get away or not? It really shouldn't be so hard."

"I think so," I say, and then I tell her she doesn't have to be so shouty about it. "My mom's coming, I think. And maybe Terrible. But they didn't notice last night when I was dead at the dinner table, so they probably won't notice if I disappear."

Nila Wister raises her eyebrows at me. "Terrible?"

"My brother, the alien."

"No wonder you are in need of a charm," she says.

I give her a look that says, You Have No Idea.

She smiles, and I don't know if she's real good at telling what different faces mean, like I am, or if it's because she's a Fortune Lady and knows everything anyway, but she says, "Being young is hard. And being old isn't any easier." Then she fingers her charms and says, "And now for the good stuff. What shall it be?"

My heart thumps in my chest as I look them over. "Where did your dad get them?"

"He never told me," she says, "and I never asked."

"Why?"

"You don't ask a magician his secrets."

"Your dad was a magician?" I say.

"Something like that."

I tell her that my dad worked in computers. And I would have asked him lots of things if I had the chance.

She brushes her hand across the charms that hang from her wheelchair, making them swing. "Take your pick."

My eyes find the butterfly charm, with its wings open, ready to fly. "And you think it will chase away the Bad Luck?"

She tilts her head to the side. "Do you doubt the Fortune Lady?"

Then I reach for the butterfly, but before I can touch it, Nila says, "Just a moment. Let me untie it first."

Her tiny fingers pull at the knotted yarn until it

comes loose. Then she rubs her thumb over the glass wings like she is saying good-bye or telling it to be good to me. Or maybe thanking it for bringing her the Good Luck for so many years. But when I ask her if that's what she's doing, she shakes her head and says, "No, I had an itchy thumb is all."

I'm not sure I believe her, but it doesn't matter because then Nila Wister puts the butterfly in my hand. "This one was my sister's," she says.

Perched in my palm, the butterfly is lighter than I thought it would be, smaller even, and I wonder how something as little as this could do anything so big as keep me from being alone.

I tell Nila I have to go, and she grabs my hands with both of hers and holds on until I look her right in the eyeballs. Her dark eyes say, You Will Help Me, Won't You? and she waits until I say that I will before she lets me go.

When she does, I slip the butterfly into my pants pocket and hurry back to Patsy Cline and the mural. I don't know how the butterfly knows what to do, because I haven't even wished on it or anything, but there, in the activity room, right beside Patsy Cline, is Vera Bogg. And she's helping.

"Look who came back," Patsy Cline says to me.

Vera holds up her paintbrush that's been dipped in purple.

"Where did you get the paint?" I ask.

Patsy Cline says, "Mr. Rodriguez."

"Don't worry," says Vera Bogg, "there's no pink."

"I'm not worried," I say, even though I kind of am.

Vera stands back and takes a long look at the mural. "This is different."

"Penelope drew a cow," says Patsy Cline, pointing up at the moon.

"I've still never heard of a cow with hearts on the outside," Vera Bogg says. "And I've never heard of a Mother Goose with mittens on either."

"Not all art has to be real-looking," I tell her, shaking my head.

"If that's so," Vera Bogg says, "then why can't Mother Goose drive a monster truck? Huh?"

And when she says those words, just then, I can almost hear Mister Leonardo say in a quiet voice, "My goodness, little darling, that pink girl over there sure does make a good point."

Good gravy. The strangest day in the world: when Leonardo da Vinci thinks that Vera Bogg has a point about art. And when I think so, too. But I decide it's better not to think about that for too long, and instead I get my No. 2 Hard drawing pencil going on the wall under Mother Goose.

"What are you doing?" Vera Bogg says to me.

"Is that a truck?" asks Patsy Cline.

"Not just a truck," I say. "A monster one."

When I finish, Vera Bogg looks at it close up and shakes her head. "A bird driving a truck. I like things that look real."

"Then, Vera Bogg," I say, smiling, "you're really not going to like this at all." And in a couple of minutes, there's an alien in a spaceship on a faraway planet.

Vera says, "Humph," and then gets back to paint-

ing the dish that runs away with the spoon. After a while she says, "So where's everybody else?"

"Mr. Rodriguez is calling them, too," I say. "But you're the first one to get here."

Vera Bogg stops painting. "But Mr. Rodriguez didn't call me."

Patsy Cline and me look at each other. "Then how come you're here?" I say.

She shrugs. "I don't know, I just got to thinking about it and figured I'd give it another try."

My eyes get big when I think that maybe, just maybe, the butterfly had something to do with this. I pat my pocket and can almost feel its wings whisper, whisper something to me.

# 16.

I keep on painting long after Patsy Cline and Vera Bogg go home. I lose track of time and don't stop until I hear Grandpa Felix's voice behind me. "Oh my," he says. "That's quite a scene."

"Grandpa Felix," I say. "What are you doing here?"

"Picking you up a half hour ago."

I tell him I'm sorry but I wanted to get as much done as I could because it has to be finished by next Saturday. And then when I notice that he is standing upright and not passed out on the floor because of the awful nursing home smell that's worse than hospitals, I say, "Hey, you're all the way inside!"

"I'm on borrowed time," he says, wiping his forehead. "Are you ready to go?"

I tell him I just have to clean up, and while I start doing that, he gets a closer look at the mural. "So, Mother Goose isn't too old and close to death to drive?"

"I guess not."

"Interesting." Grandpa Felix clears his throat. "And is this an alien? On the moon?"

I rinse the paintbrushes in the sink. "No, that's Jupiter. The other one is the moon."

"But that's an alien," he says. "Have I got that part right?"

"You do."

"My Mother Goose rhymes are a little rusty. Remind me which one is about an alien on Jupiter?"

"It's art, Grandpa." I throw the newspaper in the trash can and stick the paintbrushes in a plastic bag. "And not all art has to be real-looking, you know."

"You don't say."

I do. I do say.

"Ah, art," he says. "Don't mistake what I'm saying, little darling, I like it quite a bit." Then he says, "'Hey diddley diddle, the cat and the fiddle, the cow something something the moon. The little dog laughed, something something something, and the dish ran away with the spoon.' I never did really understand what was going on in that rhyme."

"The dog thinks the cow jumping over the moon is funny," I explain, "but the dish doesn't think so because she isn't a very happy person and so she grabs the spoon and they run away to go home."

Grandpa says, "Like I said, I never did really understand this one. But there's something very familiar about the face on that moon," he says. "I think I've seen that big nose before."

"Could be," I say. "Could be."

Grandpa touches his finger to my nose and I know we're back to being okay, thank lucky stars. Or, lucky butterfly. He puts his hand on my shoulder and walks me down the hall. He nods and says hello to the old people in the wheelchairs along the wall.

"I've been thinking," he says to me. "How about on my next shoot I let you take a picture?"

I tell him yes, yes, yes. And then I say speaking of pictures, can he can bring his camera here on Saturday now that he can stand the smell enough to be inside?

He says, "I suppose. Why?"

"Because the photographer for *The Portwaller Tribune* can't make it and I thought maybe you could take some pictures and send them in to the newspaper."

"That's not the way it generally works," he says. "And what makes you think the newspaper would want to use my pictures?"

I pat the butterfly in my pocket and say, "You have to believe, Grandpa."

He shakes his head. "Penelope Crumb."

"Grandpa Crumb," I say back.

Then he just smiles and says we need to go because this place is starting to make him feel woozy.

"You get used to the smell after a while," I say.

"Little darling," he says, "this is not a smell I particularly want to get used to."

On our way out, I stick my hand in my pocket and give the butterfly a gentle squeeze.

Littie Maple is waiting for me inside our apartment building. "I want to talk to you and your brother," she says. "Now."

She's got a look on her face that says, This Is Very Serious, so I say fine and she follows me close up the stairs. So close she steps on the backs of my shoes and almost makes me fall down the stairs and die. "I don't know if Terrible's home, Littie," I say when I get my balance again.

Littie says she saw him come upstairs a half hour ago after saying hello to some boy with a red T-shirt that says LAMBRETTAS.

"You're really good at observing," I say.

She tells me thanks, and then she follows me inside our apartment.

Terrible is on the couch watching TV. "Littie wants to talk to us," I tell him.

He keeps his eyes on the screen. "What for?"

The TV gets Littie's attention. "Is that *Max Adventure?*" she says.

Terrible says that it is, and Littie tells him she hasn't seen this episode.

"Littie," I say, "I thought you wanted to talk to us."

"Right," she says. "I do." Then she points to the TV. "Is Max lost in Canaper Valley again?"

"Only because he's blindfolded," says Terrible.

I roll my eyes at the both of them and have to wait until a commercial before Littie will tell us what's on her mind.

"I just want you to know," she says, "that I've been interviewing people in our building all day, and no one else seems to think that having a brother or a sister is all that bad."

She opens her notebook. "For example, Mr. Nix in apartment Two-C says his sister Elsie is, and I quote, 'the kindest person you could ever lay eyes on in this planet.'"

"Is she the one who leaves a basket of candy downstairs by the mailboxes?" says Terrible.

Littie says that she is, and I say, "Oh, she *is* very kind."

Littie isn't finished. "And Mrs. Mason in apartment Three-B says her brother got her to lose fifty pounds."

"That doesn't sound so nice," I say.

"Have you seen Mrs. Mason?" asks Littie. "She could do to lose another twenty, and I'm sure he was only thinking of her health. I'm just saying."

"More like forty," says Terrible. "How many people did you talk to?"

"Twelve," she says, and he groans. "That may not be a very scientific sample, but it's a start. And it confirms what I thought."

"What's that?" Terrible and me say at the same time.

Littie Maple points to a page in her notebook. "That you are weird. The both of you."

This makes Terrible laugh, which makes me laugh.

"You didn't need to interview a bunch of strangers to find that out," he says.

"Yeah, Littie," I say. "I could have told you that." I look at Terrible and say, "You're weird."

"Not half as weird as you," he says back.

And that makes us laugh even more.

I don't know what Littie Maple expected us to do, but she puts down her notebook and watches the rest of *Max Adventure* without saying a word.

# 17.

At school, the butterfly charm works so good that I don't get any notes sent home. Not even one. Not even when I forget to raise my hand before talking, twice. Because Miss Stunkel is out with the stomach flu for four whole days.

My pocket is so full of the Good Luck that there is no quiz on decimal points all week. Then, on my walk home from school one day, I find two dollars and forty-three cents, just there in the street waiting for me to notice. Which is enough to buy four orange Popsicles.

On Friday, Miss Stunkel is back. She looks a little

green, not as green as the alien in the mural, not alien-green exactly, but sick-green. And because of that green, and the Good Luck, she does a lot more sitting than standing and a lot less paying attention to me talking without raising my hand first.

I don't even see her chicken-bone finger. Not even once.

In the afternoon, Miss Stunkel looks worse. "I'm going to sit here for a bit. Who would like to share what you are doing this weekend?" she says from the back of the room.

I raise my hand. She says my name quietly, like just the feel of my name on her tongue might send her running to the bathroom. I stand up and say, "Patsy Cline and Vera Bogg and me have been working on a mural at Portwaller's Blessed Home for the Aging."

"Oh, that's right," says Miss Stunkel. "And I understand you have been leading the group, Penelope?"

That time my name seems to come out a little easier.

"Well, I was." I think about explaining how when it comes to art, people don't like other people to tell them what to do all the time. And that some people would rather see a dumb snowman than a cow with hearts. And that's just fine. But instead, I say, "Not anymore."

Miss Stunkel nods and tells me to go on.

"And tomorrow is a big party to show off what we did."

Patsy Cline says, "It's not finished yet, but holy moly, it is a dandy piece of work. And there's even a cow."

Vera Bogg agrees and says, "You should see it. Really, you should."

But I tell them they can't because the party is only for the old people who live at the home. "But there's going to be an article and picture in *The Portwaller Tribune* about it, so you can see it in the newspaper." Then I sit down.

"Thank you, Penelope," says Miss Stunkel. "I've heard from Mr. Rodriguez about what a fine job you all have done despite some challenges. You really are something." And she makes a big deal out of the *something*. It's probably just the leftover stomach bug talking, and I know she means all of us, not just me. But even so, to be *something* to Miss Stunkel is good enough luck for me.

With all this Good Luck, though, I can't help but worry that the Bad Luck is just waiting somewhere in a corner, getting ready for a sneak attack. The butterfly charm has worked real good so far, just like Nila said it would, if I believed. And I do believe. At least I think so.

But bringing Good Luck for things like finding money on the sidewalk and making Miss Stunkel be at home sick with the stomach bug is a lot different from getting kids who are mad at you to come back and finish a mural. And for helping an old lady escape from a place she doesn't want to be. How is this little butterfly supposed to do all that?

When I get to thinking about it, my heart pounds and my eyes get all blurry, and I wonder, I just wonder, if the Bad Luck is going to end up killing me dead.

Right after supper, the phone rings. Mom answers it in the kitchen and then hands the phone over to me on her way down the hall. "Patsy Cline," she tells me.

I grab the phone and shout, "Hello!" Because it's Patsy Cline, and she's calling *me*.

She says hello back and then asks if I want to spend the night and then drive over with her in the morning to Portwaller's Blessed Home for the Aging. My insides start to shake. "Mom!" I yell. "Can I spend the night at Patsy Cline's house?!"

"What? I'm in the laundry room."

I close my eyes and yell louder, as loud as I can. "CAN I SPEND THE NIGHT AT PATSY CLINE'S?"

"Penelope Rae." (Bursting appendix.) When I open my eyes, Mom is beside me, giving me a look that says, Stop Your Hollering, You Weren't Raised by Wolves.

"Can I?"

She sighs, a heavy Mom sigh that seems to go on for a year. When it's over she says, "Did you clean your room?"

Good gravy. I cover the phone with my hand

so Patsy Cline can't hear. "No," I whisper, "but it's Patsy Cline. PUUULLLLEEEAAASE let me."

Mom shakes her head at me and then says, "Clean your room first. And I mean I want the mountain of clothes that lives in the center of your room gone. And you should take a shower."

She says some other things, too, after that, but I'm already back on the phone with Patsy Cline telling her I'll be over right away.

I race to my room and grab my suitcase from the closet. I throw in some clothes from the Heap, my drawing pad and pencils, and then when I stand at my desk and can't decide whether to bring any games, or a deck of cards, or my make-your-own-jewelry kit, I bring everything.

I sit on my suitcase to snap it closed and then drag it out into the living room. "I'm ready," I say to my mom.

She says, "You didn't take a shower."

"My word. Do I have to?"

Mom gives me a look that says, You Do, in Fact. "And wash your hair."

I tell her fine and then am back in my room. I undress, throw my clothes on the Heap, and take the fastest shower in the history of getting clean. So fast, I don't use any soap and barely any water. And after I'm done I put on Mom's lotion that I find under the sink, just in case she gives me the stink test.

To my surprise, I find clothes without stains on them in a dresser drawer and I quick put them on. Then, because I know she will ask me, I clean my room. I do this by shoving the Heap into my closet. It's a lot, and my closet isn't very big, so I have to put all of my weight against the door until it closes.

"My room's clean," I tell Mom when I'm back in the living room.

"Truth?" she says.

I nod.

"The pile of clothes?"

"Gone from the center of the floor, honest to goodness," I say. "You can check if you don't believe me."

But she must believe, because she grabs her car

keys from the table by the door, and we're off to Patsy Cline's.

Patsy Cline's mom answers the door. She's got Patsy's mangy dog tucked under her arm, and I think he's happy to see me because he only tries to bite me once.

"Come on in, sugar pie," says Mrs. Watson, "and don't mind Roger here. And don't put your fingers too close to his mouth. He'll gnaw them like beef jerky." Then she calls out to Patsy Cline to let her know I'm here.

Patsy Cline hollers, "Back here, Penelope!" And so I scoot on by Roger, keeping my fingers tucked away safely in my pockets, and head for Patsy's room. I can hear her singing, *"Now keep on a walkin', keep on a talkin' / and I'll do my best to make the rest / of this lovely dream come true."* Which makes me smile, because this sure does seem like it could be a dream, thank lucky stars. But when I turn the corner and step inside her room, the dream of me and Patsy Cline being Favorites again is over.

Because there standing in the middle of Patsy

Cline's cow-print rug is Vera Bogg. She's got so many ruffles on her pink dress that I don't know where to look first. Vera tells me hi and then asks if I like her outfit because she must notice me staring. All I can do is move my head up and down because when the raw hot dog feeling sets in, you start to not be able to talk or think right.

Patsy Cline says that she and Vera are playing Singing Superstars and then asks if there is something wrong. There sure is. It begins with Vera Bogg and ends with me not being Patsy's Favorite. But this is something I don't want to say in front of Vera. So I just say, "I think I ate a bad hot dog."

"Your turn," says Vera Bogg, handing me a pretend microphone.

"I'm no singer," I say, shaking my head.

Vera shrugs and then makes up a song about me eating a bad hot dog and not wanting to sing. Patsy Cline laughs, and my cheeks burn because I don't see what's so funny.

I sit on the floor beside Patsy Cline's bed and listen to Vera's awful song. The more she sings, the more

I don't want to be here. I think even Roger must feel the same way, because halfway through the song, I hear him howl in pain.

Finally, she hands the microphone back to Patsy Cline. But soon after, they are making up duets, just the two of them. Right in front of me.

They are singing some song about two friends that like each other's shoes. So I interrupt them and say, "My friend Nila is a fortune teller."

This gets their attention. Patsy Cline says, "Who's Nila?"

"You don't know her," I say. "She's from Coney Island."

"Where's that?" says Vera Bogg.

"Some faraway place that's not made up," I say. And then I go on and on about how she comes from a carnival family and her brother is a strongman and how her picture is on posters all over the world. And how I'm her Favorite. And I make a big deal out of that last part.

"How did she learn to read fortunes?" asks Patsy Cline.

"Oh, um, her grandmother taught her after she caught a fever as a child and almost died from a spider bite," I say. Because sometimes you have to make things up to keep people's attention.

It works, too. "Wow," they say, and then they stare at me, waiting for me to tell them more. Which I do, and once I get started making things up it's pretty easy to keep going.

"Did she tell you your fortune?" Patsy asks me.

"She did," I say. And then I straighten my back and tell them that I am going to be a very non-dead famous artist like Leonardo da Vinci. Which I'm sure is what Nila Wister would tell me if she ever did tell me my fortune.

"Will she tell us ours?" asks Vera.

I shake my head. "She only does fortune telling for her Favorite these days."

"I don't want to know my fortune," says Patsy Cline. And she's got a look of worry on her face.

"*I* do," says Vera. And then she says she just knows she will live in a pink house with a matching car and a backyard full of bunny rabbits. "When can I meet this Nila person?"

"She's leaving." And that's when I realize that I won't see her again after tomorrow. Maybe never.

Patsy Cline asks me where she's going, but I can't answer. Because all I can think about now is what it will be like to be Nila Wister's Favorite when she doesn't live in Portwaller anymore. If I'll still be her Favorite even. I won't be able to bring her candies, and she won't be able to ask me for them. She will be gone, back to some dream place, but without her sister, and without me.

# 18.

My big nose wakes me up the next morning. For a second or two, I can't figure out exactly what I'm smelling. But once my brains catch up to my nose, I know. Fried onions.

And I go dead, all the way dead this time, right there on Patsy Cline's cow-print rug.

I don't know how long I'm dead for, but it must be for a long while because the next thing I know, Patsy Cline is pulling at my arm and singing a song about getting up in the morning. I open my eyes and when I see Patsy Cline smiling at me as she sings, I wonder if this is heaven. But then I hear Vera Bogg's voice and know it isn't.

"Come on," says Vera Bogg. "We're running late."

"Running for what?" I say. Because when you get alive again so early in the morning after being dead, you don't really know what's going on.

"The mural!" says Patsy Cline.

I scramble to my feet but the fried onion smell almost knocks me down again. And I wonder how the Bad Luck found me. I find my pants and reach into the pocket for my butterfly, but it's not there. I check the other pockets, but come up empty. "My charm!" I say.

"What's wrong?" says Patsy Cline and Vera Bogg at the same time.

I open my suitcase and take everything out. Oh no. Oh no. Oh no.

Patsy Cline asks what I'm looking for, and when I tell her a good-luck charm, she says, "What do you need that for?"

I don't know what kind of a question that is, because what does anyone need a good-luck charm for, anyway? "For good luck," I say.

She shakes her head at me like I'm being silly. But I know better.

"Don't you smell that?" I whisper.

"You mean Mom's meatloaf?"

I sniff again and wince. That is not meatloaf, it's not, and if they can't smell those horrible fried onions, then I know the Bad Luck must be here only for me.

Vera Bogg says in a quiet voice to Patsy Cline, but not so quiet that I can't hear, "Maybe your mom should call a doctor."

Patsy Cline ignores her and says, "What does the charm look like?"

I tell them it's a butterfly and that it's made of glass.

"Aww," says Vera Bogg. "That sounds real pretty. Where did you get it?"

My word. I don't answer her and instead start

looking under Patsy Cline's rug, under her bed, behind her curtains, in her trash can.

"Where was the last place you saw it?" asks Patsy Cline.

I try to remember. I really do, but the Bad Luck smell is choking me and making my brain feel fuzzy. I tap my brains with my fingertips and think hard. "I was at home, in my room, packing my suitcase, and . . ."

"And what?" says Patsy Cline.

And then I remember. It was in the pocket of my other pants before I took a shower. "Oh."

"What?" says Patsy Cline. "Do you know where it is?"

I nod. "The Heap."

Mrs. Watson knocks on the door to Patsy Cline's room and tells us we need to get a move on now.

Patsy Cline tells her that I left something at home. "Can we stop by her apartment on the way?"

Mrs. Watson looks at me and frowns. "We could if we weren't running late and if you didn't live in the opposite direction of where we're headed, honey pie. What did you forget?"

"A good-luck charm," I say.

"What do you need that for?" asks Mrs. Watson. But before I can tell her, she says not to worry and that she'll call my mom and ask her to bring it with her today. "How does that sound?"

I tell her that sounds okay, and I should feel better, but I don't.

It's a long walk from Mrs. Watson's car into Portwaller's Blessed Home for the Aging. Antler Lady at the front desk is on the phone and nods at the three of us when we come in. I've got my big nose sniffing the air for any trace of fried onions to see if it's followed me from Patsy Cline's. Because without the charm in my pocket, all sorts of bad things could happen.

"I hope the others come back," says Patsy Cline as we walk past the front desk.

"Me too," says Vera Bogg.

I shake my head and think of the butterfly charm. "They won't," I say. "Not if the Bad Luck has anything to do with it."

"I don't believe in bad luck," says Vera Bogg.

"Me neither," says Patsy Cline.

"Then why have all these bad things been happening?" I ask.

Patsy Cline says, "What bad things?"

I tell her about Miss Stunkel and the notes home, and the bump in the road that made me lose Crispy Sticky, and the kids quitting the mural, and my eyelash blowing away. And other things like my brother the alien. And my dad being Graveyard Dead. And losing Favorites.

"She's got a point," says Vera Bogg. "That's a lot of bad stuff."

Patsy Cline touches my arm and says, "That's not bad luck. That's just the way things are."

"Then what about the awful smell this morning?" I say.

"What smell?"

"The one in your house that smelled like fried onions."

"Fried onions," says Patsy Cline. "Mom puts them on top of her meatloaf."

"I don't know," I say. "If there isn't any bad luck, then there can't be any good luck. And I want to believe in the Good Luck."

I hear voices from the activity room, and when me and Patsy Cline and Vera get there, my mouth falls open. Marcus, Alexander, and Birgit are there, already painting. Mr. Rodriguez, too.

"Look at that," says Patsy Cline, smiling.

I don't know if she means the mural or that the rest of the group is here, but it doesn't matter because just look.

Marcus is putting something on the truck that looks like an antenna. Alexander is painting a robot on Jack Be Nimble's T-shirt. And Birgit is putting the last of the color on a rainbow unicorn that is shooting sparkles out of its horn.

The three of them look up at us, and then just at me. I don't know what to say, because half of me is still scared about the Bad Luck, and the other half can't believe that the rest of the kids came back to finish the mural. Even without my charm.

Just then, two old men and one old lady are in the

doorway of the activity room and they peek inside. "Would you look at that," one man says. "There's a bird in a truck. Now that's something you don't see every day."

"That's Mother Goose," says the old lady, nodding.

"Nice ride," says the other.

Alexander holds up a paintbrush dipped in blue and says, "Penelope, what color do you think this robot should be?"

I'm about to tell him that whatever color he wants is fine by me, but that a blue robot would really be the best. But then I look at the three old people in the doorway. And I know it's not up to me. The mural is really for them, it's all for them. So I ask.

They look at one another, the old people do, and finally the lady says how about blue?

Alexander and me smile, and I tell her that's what I was going to say.

Vera Bogg smiles and says, "They like it. Even if there isn't any pink."

I roll my eyes. "Oh, Vera Bogg." Then I unfold

a stack of newspapers on the table next to the paint and grab the red and white tubes. I squeeze them onto the newspaper and mix them together with a paintbrush until I start to get that raw hot dog feeling. "Here," I say to her. "Pink."

Vera says, "Whoa, baby," and grabs a paintbrush, cupping one hand under the bristles, so as not to lose one drop of pink.

When the mural is finally finished, Mr. Rodriguez claps his hands and says, "You guys have done a righteous job. All of you. People will start arriving soon for the official unveiling, so just hang tight until then."

All of a sudden I'm nervous. Stomach sick, tongue-swelling nervous. All that good luck: the kids coming back, finishing the mural in time, the old people liking it (three of them, anyway). With all that good stuff, I just know the Bad Luck can't be far away.

Patsy Cline and Vera are admiring Little Bo Peep's sheep, which is now all pink. I tap Patsy Cline on the shoulder. "Do you think your mom called my mom?"

"She said she was going to," she says. "I'm sure she did."

"Okay."

"What more good luck do you need for today, anyway?" she asks me. "The mural is already done, and it looks dandy."

I want to tell her about Nila Wister for real, about what she asked me to help her do. But I know I'm not supposed to tell, that this is something that has to stay between Favorites. And I wonder if being Nila's Favorite is going to be harder than I thought. Because right now, getting Nila Wister out of here feels like a job for a muscleman, someone who is used to lifting the world over his head. And Favorite or not, I can't lift much more than a paintbrush. Especially without my charm.

# 19.

People arrive with a chocolate cake and red punch, and Mr. Rodriguez is busy directing them where to put it. Patsy Cline and Vera Bogg are back to talking about the mural again, and when Vera says she doesn't know why the farmer's wife would cut off the tails of the Three Blind Mice anyway and isn't that cruel, I slip away.

I head for the front desk because maybe Antler Lady will let me use the phone. "Excuse me," I say to her. "I need to call my mom."

She tucks one side of her angel-winged hair behind her ear and that's when I notice she's got a name tag on her chest that says ARLENE. With those antlers, I think she looks more like a Tina, but I decide to keep that to myself.

"Of course," says Arlene. She pushes the phone closer to me and says, "There you are."

Mom doesn't answer. I hang up and tell Arlene I need to try another number. Maybe Patsy Cline's mom can tell me if she talked to my mom and told her to bring the butterfly in my pants pocket in the Heap in my closet over here, pronto. But before I can do that, Grandpa Felix is here to take our picture.

"There's the artist," he says. Only he says it funny like he's from somewhere else other than Portwaller. He holds up his camera bag. "Are you ready for your close-up?"

I shrug.

"What's wrong?" he says. "Nerves got you?"

I tell him that my nerves have got me bad, and he says, "I'd be worried if they didn't. This is a big day."

But he has no idea how big.

Then Grandpa Felix takes one of the cameras he's

got around his neck and hands it over to me. "Here you go."

"What for?"

"I promised the next time you could take a picture, didn't I?" he says, winking at me.

I throw my arms around his middle and squeeze. Partly because I'm excited to finally take a picture, but mostly because I need something to hold tight to. Grandpa has to pry my arms loose, and when he does, I lead him to the activity room, where I tell Mr. Rodriguez that my grandpa is here to take our picture. Mr. Rodriguez smiles big and then waves his arms to herd us together. The next thing I know, we're all standing in front of the mural smiling and saying, "Beans."

By this time the nurses are wheeling the old people into the room, and some are walking on their own. I have to go see about Nila Wister, because this is when I'm supposed to get away. But when I turn around to leave, I run straight into my mom and Terrible.

"Did you bring it?" I say.

Mom says, "Mrs. Watson called me about some butterfly charm?"

I hold my hands out. "Where? Where is it?"

"I don't know, Penelope," she says. "I couldn't find it." Then she tells me it wasn't in my pants pocket, wasn't in the pile of clothes that was supposed to have been picked up either, Missy. And not in my closet, which is a giant mess. Sorry, she says. And by the way, no more anything until that closet is clean.

I don't know how she can think of clean closets at a time like this.

Terrible looks at the mural. "How'd that giant bird get a driver's license, anyway?"

I shake my head at him and say, "I have to do something."

Up until now, me helping Nila escape was as real as Mother Goose driving a truck, as real as unicorns with sparkles, as real as aliens on Jupiter: not very. But now that it's here, I just don't know. I want to find a corner to hide in and tell the Bad Luck to come find me once and for all. Then maybe I wouldn't have to do this.

On the way to Nila's room, I find a small corner behind a fern in the hallway, and I squat there and wait. "Here I am," I say to the Bad Luck. "It's me, Penelope Crumb. Come find me because I can't take your sneak attacks."

I don't know how long I'm here, but the Bad Luck doesn't show up. Nila Wister does. She tells the nurse who's pushing her chair to leave her here, that she's going to visit awhile here with her new friend. Which I think is me.

After the nurse leaves, Nila says, "What in the name of Pete are you doing back there?" And before I can answer, she says, "I've been waiting for you. Come on. We've got to get moving." She points down the hall. "This way. I need to get some things from my room."

I get to my feet and before I have the chance to think, I'm pushing her, and we're going.

"I was beginning to think you're the kind of girlie who says one thing and does another," she says to me.

"I don't know what kind of girlie I am exactly."

"You are the kind that's going to help me get out of here," she says.

When we get to her room, she tells me to fetch her bag from the closet. Then she points to the dresser and has me open the drawers and stuff all her clothes into the bag. She doesn't have much, nothing like the Heap, and even though I'm stuffing as fast as I can, she's telling me to hurry up about it.

Grandpa's camera swings around my neck as I empty her drawers. "You don't have to be so bossy," I tell her. When I'm done, she leans down over the bag and pulls the zipper closed.

"There's something about the sound of a zipper," she says. And she's smiling.

"You have teeth," I say. "I've never seen them before."

She taps them with her fingernail and then clicks them together. "And they're all mine, too. No falsies."

"I want to take your picture," I say, holding Grandpa's camera up to my eye. "So I can remember you."

Nila rubs her hands together. "All right, but make it quick."

She looks up at me, and I tell her to say "beans." When she does, I snap her picture. "Okay, now one more just in case."

"What?"

"A good photographer always takes more than one," I tell her. "That's what Grandpa Felix does."

She tells me to be quick now, and I take another. And when I look at Nila through the camera's view-finder this time, she looks so fragile. Like her bones are made of butterfly glass.

"Do you want to take one of me?" I say. "I can mail it to you."

"What for?" she says.

"Because I'm your Favorite," I say. "And so you can remember what I look like when you're back home in Coney Island."

I shove the camera at her and then I turn my head to the side and smile. So she has a good view of my big nose. Which is my favorite feature. After two clicks, she hands the camera back to me and says, "Now let's blow this Popsicle stand."

I lift the bag onto the back of her chair, and hang

the strap across the handles. Then I grip the back of her wheelchair and we go. Every time a nurse passes us by, I stop, worried that we're going to get caught.

"Just act like we aren't doing anything wrong," she tells me.

"Are we doing something wrong?" I whisper.

"No. We. Are. Not." But then she says, "It depends on who you ask. Another person might have a different opinion on the matter."

All of a sudden, I want to know if fourth graders can go to prison. The Fortune Lady must be able to read my brain thoughts because she says, "And you're not going to jail. My goodness, it's not like we're robbing a bank or anything. Besides, you've got your charm. Nothing bad is going to happen to you."

"I have to tell you something," I say, stopping once again.

"What's that?"

"I don't have the butterfly charm with me."

"Don't tell me you lost it," she says.

"No, it's at home in the Heap," I say. "I think it is, anyway."

"Big mistake," she says, shaking her head. And then says that she doesn't know what a Heap is but it sounds like a place where things go to get buried. "No matter, I've got mine, so that should keep the good luck on my side."

But she doesn't say what it will do for my side. And when I tell her that, Nila Wister says, "Luck will find you." Then she points her old finger toward the other end of the hall. "Now we've got to go."

I push her past the nurses' station toward the activity room. I smile at the busy nurses and put a look on my face that says, Don't Worry, She's Just Going for a Walk and Not Leaving Forever. It works, because nobody stops us and asks me where I'm taking her.

"Now wait here for a minute," Nila Wister tells me. "We have to make sure the busybody who sits out front isn't there. You go check."

"Arlene," I say.

"Who?"

"The busybody," I say. "She let me use the phone." I tiptoe around the corner. Nobody is at the desk, and the path to the front door is clear. "She's not there," I tell Nila when I get back to her.

"Good," she says. "Let's go."

"Don't you want to say good-bye to anybody?" I ask.

She's quick to say no. "Nobody here will even know I'm gone."

And I know what she means. I push her past the activity room, past the crowd, past the mural, past my mom and Grandpa Felix and Terrible, who don't look like they're missing me at all.

"Fast now," says Nila. She's pointing toward the front door. "Go, girl, go!"

I start to run. Here we go, and pretty soon me and Nila Wister are speeding toward the door. The door is an automatic, so I slow my legs until it opens for us. "Don't slow down!" she yells.

"Stop bossing," I say again, and I steer her through the open door and out onto the street.

My heart is pounding in my chest, and I don't know if it's from pushing this wheelchair or because we just made it outside and now what?

Nila cranes her neck around to look at the door. "We're out, we're out. And nobody saw us." Then she gives out a little whoop. "Don't stop now," she says. "Get me to the bus stop down the block."

"My arms are tired."

She tells me I'm young and that she hardly weighs more than a loaf of bread. I get her going again, and the farther we get from Portwaller's Blessed Home for the Aging, the more I can feel the Bad Luck around the corner. "I don't know about this," I say.

Nila leans forward in her chair. "Come on, come on."

The cars on the street blow past us as I try to slow my heart. I look behind to see if anybody's coming after us. And truth be told, I wish someone would. But nobody does, and even with Nila, my new Favorite, right here with me, I can't help but feel really very alone. "Where are you going to go?" I say.

"I told you," says Nila. "Home. Can't you push me any faster?"

"Coney Island?"

"Home," she says.

"But what for?"

"My life," she tells me.

I stop. And that's when I remember. "Your posters, Nila! Did you forget them?"

Nila doesn't say anything for a long while and then holds on to her acorn charm and whispers something I can't hear.

"Nila?"

She sighs and says, "It's all right. Leave them."

"But they're your life," I remind her. "You said so." I look behind us, down the street. "We're so close. I can go back." And I don't wait for her to tell me no, because I know Nila wants those posters, I know it, and I wouldn't be much of a Favorite if I didn't go get them.

# 20.

When I take off running, I can hear Nila Wister shout at me, "Big mistake!" But I keep going. Fast. Because when you don't have your charm in your pocket, the only thing you can do is try to outrun the Bad Luck.

I run past slow people on the sidewalk, weaving in between them, and I dart around a lady with a stroller and then a dog walker. I'm nearly flattened by the stroller and eaten by a pack of poodles, but somehow I make it back to Portwaller's Blessed alive, thank lucky stars.

I stop to get my breath at the front door, but I

don't stand still for too long. And then after I put a look on my face that says, I Definitely Did Not Just Help an Old Lady Escape, I go inside.

A crowd of people are gathered around Arlene's desk and they all stare at me when I come in. "I didn't do anything," I say, trying to act all normal and not like I just stole an old lady in a wheelchair.

"That's her," says Arlene to one of the men in the crowd. And she's pointing at me.

I want to say it's not polite to point and then go about my business, but then Mom and Terrible and Grandpa Felix are here and they ask me where I've been.

"Outside," I say.

"You are so in trouble," says Terrible.

I guess our crowd starts to get noticed, because the next thing I know, Patsy Cline and Vera Bogg and Mr. Rodriguez are here, too. And Patsy Cline says, "What's all the fuss?"

Then a man in a suit tells me he wants to talk. He looks like he might be from NASA, but when I ask him if he's on alien business, he says he doesn't know what I'm talking about and would I please sit down on the couch. This is code for Yes I Am. I'm pretty sure.

"Do I have to?" I say, because I've got an old lady out in the street by herself with non-working legs, and it's not really a good time for alien talk.

The man almost smiles, but my mom doesn't at all. She tells me she wants me to sit down and answer this man's questions, Right Now. I look toward the front door, wondering what Nila Wister must be thinking. Now that the Bad Luck has found me and she's out there alone.

I sit down, facing the door, and the man sits beside me. He says his name is Martin, and he has a regular-size nose that isn't very stand-out at all. The kind that you wouldn't notice if you saw him on the street, and that's really too bad.

He says he's Portwaller's Blessed administrator and wants to know what I did with Nila Wister.

"You mean you're like the Boss?"

He nods. "I guess you could say that."

"I was a Boss for a couple of days," I tell him. "It's hard work."

He says it sure is. And then maybe because he's a Boss too or because I'm so tired after pushing Nila in her wheelchair, or because I'm kind of relieved I don't have to go through with helping Nila escape, I take a deep breath and tell him everything. About the Bad Luck, about the charms, and about Nila Wister.

Martin says he's mostly interested in the fact that Nila Wister is safe and sitting in her wheelchair just around the corner. He doesn't so much want to talk about the charms or the Bad Luck. But if he doesn't know that the Bad Luck is out there somewhere, ready for the sneak attack, then I guess I'm not going to be the one to tell him.

Then, when he sends somebody outside to bring back Nila Wister, I tell him that she wants to go home. "She doesn't have any friends here," I say. "Just me."

"Nila Wister?" says Patsy Cline. "The fortune teller?"

Vera Bogg says, "She's an old person?"

I nod and Patsy Cline crinkles up her nose like

she's trying to remember everything that I said about Nila and trying to figure out whether or not I made it all up.

"Do you think she would tell me my fortune?" says Vera Bogg.

Good gravy.

After that, Mr. Rodriguez tells Patsy Cline and Vera Bogg that whatever is going on is not their concern and then he leads them back to the mural party. Which is where I would very much like to be.

"Why did you do this?" Mom asks, with a look on her face that says, This Is a Hundred Times Worse Than a Note from Miss Stunkel.

"Nila asked me to," I say. "She needed my help. And I am her Favorite."

"Favorite what?" asks Grandpa Felix.

But before I can answer him, Nila Wister comes rolling in through the front door. And she looks like a fish that's been reeled in too close to suppertime.

"Nila," I say, going to her. I kneel beside her wheelchair and in a low voice tell her I'm sorry, very sorry, she didn't get to go home but that everything is going to be okay because she can still be my Favorite, and now that she's here we'll still be able to see each other. And I say it's going to be okay over and over and that I'm sorry I didn't have my charm.

She doesn't look at me, and her fingers are wrapped tight around her acorn charm. She's wishing I would just go away, that we all would, or that she would. I'm pretty sure. Finally she says, "I told you not to come back." And she says it in a way that I know I'm not her Favorite anymore.

Martin comes over to us and taps me on my shoulder. He tells me he's done with me, and that he wants to talk to Nila alone.

"Is she in trouble?" I say.

Mom pulls on my arm before he has a chance to answer me, and the next thing I know, I'm in the car and we're going home.

It takes me the rest of the day to find the butterfly charm in the Heap. But I do find it, thank lucky stars, and when I do, I make a wish on it. For Nila.

# 21.

Days later, Grandpa Felix is knocking on our door. When I open it, he says he has a surprise so gather around. On Regular days, I like surprises, but I haven't had a Regular day in a while, so I tell him I'm not so sure I'm up for it.

"Nonsense," he says and tells me to follow. He hollers for Mom and Terrible and when we're all here in the kitchen, Grandpa Felix slaps a copy of *The Portwaller Tribune* in the center of the table. "Page C-three," he says.

Mom quickly opens the newspaper, fumbling through the pages, and then gives a squeal and lays the paper out flat. There, on the page, is a picture of the mural and us in front of it. "Look at that!" she says.

Grandpa tells Mom to read the article out loud. She does. It says all about me and the rest of the kids wanting to paint a mural that the residents of Portwaller's Blessed Home for the Aging can enjoy and about how Mr. Rodriguez organized the whole thing. "Oh," says Mom, "Penelope, your name is right here!"

My face gets hot. "It doesn't say anything about me trying to steal Nila Wister, does it?"

Mom shakes her head, and Terrible says that information would be in the police blotter in a completely different section of the newspaper. Then he laughs.

"But that's not all," says Grandpa Felix. He turns the page, and there, staring back at me, is Nila Wister. And beside her picture, the picture that I took of her, there's a whole other article: "Fortune Teller Charms Portwaller."

Grandpa Felix says when he got to looking at the

pictures he took for the mural party, he saw the ones I took of Nila Wister and then talked to the reporter at the newspaper. "I told him a little bit about her, as much as I knew, and I guess he was interested in doing a story. He must have interviewed her this week and wanted to run the stories together." Then Grandpa reaches into his pocket and pulls out an envelope of money. "Here's your share," he says to me, handing it over.

"She gets paid?" says Terrible.

I don't know what to say because my first thought is that now I can have orange Popsicles any time I want. And my second thought has to do with Nila Wister.

Grandpa says, "Okay, moneybags, are you ready to go? The wedding is across town, so we'll need to get going sooner than later."

I look from Terrible to Grandpa. "Do you think he could be your assistant today?"

Grandpa raises his eyebrows at me. And Terrible does the same. They almost look alike. "Okay by me," says Grandpa, smiling.

Terrible says, "I just have to get my jacket," and then he's up from the table. He pulls on my ponytail as he goes by me and says, "Even for an old lady stealer, you're okay sometimes."

I give him a look that says, Even for an Alien, You're Not the Worst Sometimes. Then I ask Grandpa Felix, "Is Portwaller's Blessed Home for the Aging on the way?"

Grandpa says that it is and that he'll take me there as long as I promise not to try to kidnap any more old people and as long as he doesn't have to go inside.

"It's not polite to call them old, Grandpa," I say. And then I ask if we can stop at Ernie's Go-Mart first. "There's something I need to buy."

Arlene at the front desk is not very happy to see me. She gives me the Stink Eye when I come in and says, "I'll be watching you, young lady. So no funny business."

I tell her okay and that I'm just here for a visit, that's all. I swing the plastic bag I got from Ernie's Go-Mart and say, "Honest to goodness."

She says, "Humph," and then nothing else. I head

down the hall toward Nila Wister's room. Her door is partway open, so I knock and peek my head in.

Nila is in her wheelchair with her back to me. I set down the plastic bag and then whisper her name. When she doesn't answer, I whisper her name again and tiptoe up to her chair so as not to scare her to death. She doesn't move, not even a little, so I get my finger ready to poke her in the face. "Don't you dare," she says, making me jump.

"You're awake."

"Of course I am," she says. "And you need to work on your tiptoeing. I heard you coming before you even got up this morning."

I go around to the front of her chair. She looks tiny, like the world is getting ready to swallow her down. "I'm sorry you didn't get to go home," I say.

"I know you are," she says. "You told me a dozen times when they brought me back."

Then she flaps her lips at me and says, "Yes, well. That's how luck would have it, I guess."

"The Bad Luck," I say.

"The very same."

Nila Wister looks at me for a long time with those dark eyes, looks deep inside me for the reason that I'm here. I know I'm not her Favorite anymore, if I ever really was, and since I'm not, I reach into my pocket and pull out the butterfly charm. "Here," I say, holding it out to her.

She cocks her head to the side. "You don't want it?"

"You should keep it," I say. "Since you're still here and all." And because if that was the only thing I had from my dead sister, if I had a dead sister, I'd want to hold on to it. Not so much for luck, but just because.

Nila Wister closes her hand around the butterfly and maybe makes a wish to go home again, I'm not sure.

So I ask, "Are you going to try to leave again?"

She flaps her lips at me. "Not today. I've had my fill of leaving for now." Then she looks at the poster of the Fortune Lady, the one above her dresser, and she says, "This isn't how I wanted to end up."

"You mean here in Portwaller?"

She shakes her head, and then I know she means she didn't want to end here, like this.

"But you're not alone," I tell her. "There are an awful lot of people here who didn't want you to go. Me, for example. And I know you don't have your sister anymore, but even without your Favorite, that doesn't mean you're all alone."

She smiles at me, that Nila Wister does, and it's a smile that makes me understand even if I'm not someone's Favorite, *I'm* not alone. Grandpa and Mom and Terrible and Patsy Cline were all here to see the mural, here to find me when I took Nila, here with me now. And Favorite or not, that is lucky. I'm pretty sure.

Then I pick up my bag from Ernie's Go-Mart and pull out the newspaper article. "Look," I say, pointing to her picture. "It's all about you."

Nila holds the newspaper close to her old eyeballs and squints. When she's done reading, she places it on her lap and says, "Well, that's something."

I tell her that it is something, it's a lot of something actually, and before I can say more, two old ladies are at Nila's door asking if she wants to come down to the ice cream social in the activity room.

"Oh, I don't think so," says Nila.

"It's *ice cream*, Nila," I whisper.

The ladies smile at me, and then at Nila, and then at me, like they've never heard anybody turn down ice cream before and therefore don't know what to say. And after a while of nobody saying anything, I take charge and say, "She'll be down in a minute."

They smile and nod and shuffle away.

Nila says now look who's being so bossy. I raise my eyebrows at her and say, "You've got some new friends."

"They must've seen my picture in the paper."

"That's the picture I took, you know," I tell her. Because even if she has new friends, she shouldn't forget about me.

"I know it," she says. "And it's not a bad one. Even for an old lady."

"A fortune lady."

"How about that," she says, rubbing her thumb over the butterfly.

"Oh, and there's something else," I say. I hand her the plastic bag.

Her old, bony fingers pull open the bag and she gives me a look that says, What Are You Up To? before sticking her nose inside. Then she looks up at me, and when she does, she's got on such a grin. She pulls out a chocolate bar, one that I bought with the money from her newspaper picture.

"I can bring you one every time I come to visit now," I tell her.

Nila Wister holds the candy bar up to her nose. When she does, her eyes go closed for a long while, like she's remembering a dream, or maybe remembering her sister, or something else.

And when she finally opens them, they sparkle like butterfly glass. Then she whispers, "My Favorite."

"I thought orange was your Favorite," I say.

She scrunches up her shoulders and says, "Ah, that was before. This is my new Favorite. Things don't always stay the same, you know." Like that could be a good thing.

I tell her I know, but that the way things are now is okay by me.

She winks at me, that Nila Wister does, and she says, "I have something for you, too. In the first drawer of that bedside table over there."

I go over to the table and pull open the drawer. There's nothing in it except for my paintbrush lying on top of my crinkled paper bag. I give my paintbrush a quick squeeze and slip it into my back pocket. Then I take out the bag and unfold it. Somehow the stain doesn't look so much like a foot with a missing toe anymore. If you look at it a certain way, and make your eyes go kind of squinty, it looks almost like a star. And when I tell Nila this, she says, "Maybe you just found yourself a good-luck charm."

I fold the bag real carefully, because it's not every day you find that a stain changes from a foot to a star, not every day you find some luck. And as I grip the handles of Nila Wister's wheelchair and push her out the door, I wonder if maybe after all this, maybe the Good Luck found me.

Turn the page for a peek at the next book

starring PENELOPE CRUMB!

# 1.

oday I am an elephant. In a costume that I made all by myself out of my mom's old gray sweat suit stuffed with pillows because it's Be an Animal Day at school. I painted a lion on the back of the shirt because when you're in the fourth grade you never know what's going to leap out at you from behind the bushes.

As I put on my paper-towel-tube elephant nose, plump my ears, and paint my hair and face gray, I think how nice it is to be something else in the mirror for a change. When my mom pokes her head in my room and tells me I'm going to be late and asks what's the deal with the lion, I say, "Portwaller Elementary can be a real jungle."

Walking to school from our apartment is only a couple of blocks, but when you're an elephant, for some reason, it seems to take a long time to get there. Plus there's all the strange looks you get on the way. The kind of looks that say Do You Know What You Look Like? I just smile at them in a way that means Yes Indeed I Am Supposed to Look This Way, I've Done So on Purpose And Not by Accident. More than a couple of people shout at me and offer me peanuts, but I just pretend they are the strange ones. I'm an excellent pretender.

But when I finally get to Portwaller Elementary, I know something is wrong as soon as I step inside: I'm the only animal at the zoo.

All of the other kids, and I mean ALL of them, are in normal, everyday school kind of clothes without a single tail or paw or beak. I start to elephant-sweat as everybody begins to stare at me, and when I wipe my forehead, some of the gray paint comes off on my fingers. Good gravy.

I see my used-to-be-best-friend, Patsy Cline Roberta Watson, at the drinking fountain. We're still friends, just not best ones anymore, mostly because of a girl called Vera Bogg who doesn't wear anything but pink. Which is something I will never understand.

When I go up to Patsy Cline, my elephant nose brushes against her hair and she screams and spits water all down her shirt. I tell her it's me, it's me, Penelope Crumb, but her shirt is already soaked and she's got a look on her face that says Don't You Know I'm Allergic to Things with Tails?

"Why aren't you dressed like an animal?" I say.

Then she says, "The real question is why are you?"

And when I remind her about Be an Animal Day, she shakes her head at me and says this: "You've got the date wrong, Penelope. It's two Mondays from now. And did you paint your hair?"

"No, it's today," I tell her.

"I'm sure that it's not," she says.

"No," I say, "today." Because it is. It has to be.

Patsy Cline turns me around by the shoulders so I can see all the kids without tails, and then she says: "Do you see anyone else that looks like you?"

This is a trick question, of course, because even if I wasn't dressed like an elephant I wouldn't see anybody that looks like me. I wouldn't. For one thing, my big nose.

Even so, as I look at everybody else, I see that Patsy Cline has a point. Good gravy, I'm the only elephant in the room.

I take off my elephant nose and look down at the rest of me. Gray, wrinkly, pillowy. I tell Patsy Cline that it could be worse, that I was thinking about being an ostrich, but then she points to my face and says, "What are you going to do about that? And your . . ."

But before she can finish, the bell rings and we're supposed to be in Miss Stunkel's classroom. "Come on," she says, pulling at my sleeve, "we're going to get hollered at."

But hollering isn't what worries me. It's showing up in Miss Stunkel's class all gray in the face and elephanty on a Regular Day and Miss Stunkel will say that I'm Quite the Riotous Disruption and send another note home. I'm pretty sure.

Patsy Cline doesn't want to help, I can tell. But I'm still holding on to her arm, and I guess she figures she doesn't have much choice, seeing how I'm not letting go, so she pushes down the handle to the water fountain and shoves my head into the stream. "Wash it off quick," she tells me.

I splash the water on my face and scrub with my hands until I see the gray paint begin to pool around the drain. Then I lift out my drippy head, keeping my eyes shut. "Did I get it off?"

"Some of it," says Patsy Cline. "But there's a good bit left. You need some soap. And a scrub brush. And there's no time to get you to the bathroom."

"I've got paint in my eyes," I say, after opening and then shutting them real fast.

"You need a towel."

I lean in toward her so she can dry my face, but I'm still drippy when she says, "I don't have a towel. Why would I have a towel?"

So, I have no choice but to take one of the pillows from my shirt and wipe my face with it. And when I'm done, Patsy Cline looks me over and says, "Oh dear." Which is not what I was hoping for. Then she tells me we've got to go pronto and pulls me down the hall to Miss Stunkel's classroom.

When we get there, I wonder if there is ever a place an elephant can hide. If there is, it isn't in Miss Stunkel's classroom, because I can feel everybody's eyeballs on me, even Angus Meeker, who lives to get me in trouble.

Vera Bogg: "Why are you dressed like a fat chimney sweep?"

Angus Meeker: "This is going to be good."

Patsy Cline: "It's just a mix-up. She's an elephant. Chimney sweeps don't have tails. Show her your tail, Penelope."

Me: "Patsy Cline, you are not helping."

All the while, Miss Stunkel is watching me from the front of the room while she pets the Monday lizard pin that hangs from her sweater. But to my surprise, she doesn't say anything to me about my painted face or hair, my stained and wrinkly gray sweat suit, or my tail. Instead, she just says, "Penelope Crumb and Patsy Cline, you do know that when the bell rings I expect you to be in your seats?"

Me and Patsy Cline say that we do indeed and that we're awful sorry. And then Miss Stunkel tells us, not just me and Patsy Cline, but tells everybody, to open our science books so we can learn about the solar system. The solar system! Miss Stunkel's going to talk about planets and moons, thank lucky stars, and doesn't have a thing to say about Penelope Crumb, Riotous Disruptor.

I pull out my science book from my desk with a smile on my gray mess of a face, eager to hear about stardust or moon craters or whatever outer spaciness that Miss Stunkel wants to make us learn. But then, I get to wondering why it is that Miss Stunkel hasn't said anything about Elephant Me. It's not that I want her to, believe me. I don't. But because she hasn't, it starts me thinking: Why?

Miss Stunkel tells us to read the paragraph in our books called "Interesting Moon Factoids." After the diameter, mass, and average distance from Earth, there is one interesting factoid that gets my attention:

*There is no dark side of the moon. Both sides of the moon get the same amount of sunlight, but only one side of the moon is ever visible from Earth.*

Right away I get to thinking how it doesn't seem fair that we only get to see one side of the moon from here. There's more to the moon than just that one side, and what if it was having a bad day or got its Mondays mixed up and that's all that people could see and not any of the good stuff.

Miss Stunkel must be able to tell what I'm thinking somehow because she says, "Is there a problem, Penelope?"

I say, "Not really a problem, I guess. I was just wondering something."

"Let's hear it," she says.

I shake my head and look at everyone else, who is already looking back at me. "Well . . ."

"Come on now," Miss Stunkel says. "I'm sure we'd all like to hear."

Patsy Cline gives me a look that says I'm Sure You Should Keep Your Mouth Shut. But I can't help it, I have to know why Miss Stunkel hasn't said anything about me being an elephant. "Well, I was just wondering if you noticed that I'm not myself today."

Miss Stunkel says that as a matter of fact she did.

"Oh," I say.

"Is there something else, Penelope?"

"And I was also wondering," I say, "why you didn't say anything."

Patsy Cline puts her head on her desk.

Miss Stunkel takes a deep breath, and her eyeballs bounce up and down like she's trying to search her brains for just the right words. She starts to say something a couple of times but then stops herself. Finally, she says, "Let's just say that *this*," and then she waggles her finger at me, the one that looks like a boiled chicken leg dipped in nail polish, the one that has been known to cause night terrors, "whatever *this* is called, falls within what I have come to expect of you, Penelope Crumb."

I'm not sure what that means exactly, but it sounds pretty bad. And I wish that lion on the back of my shirt would wake up and show its teeth or something. But it doesn't.

And in case you missed them, be sure to check out
these other great books in the PENELOPE CRUMB series!

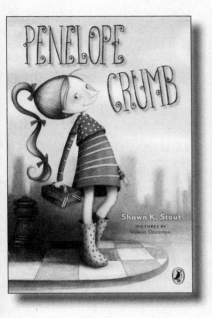

# ACKNOWLEDGMENTS

I am middle-of-the-road superstitious: I throw salt over my shoulder when I'm cooking and never ever walk under ladders, but I will let black cats cross my path (on occasion) and often step on cracks without thinking twice. But I do one hundred percent, wholeheartedly believe in luck and am in constant pursuit of finding the good kind.

My efforts in this pursuit so far have been fruitful, as I have had the great fortune of gaining the friendship and encouragement of some amazing people, in particular the DC VCFAers: Mary Quattlebaum, Jessica Leader, Winifred Conkling, Tami Lewis Brown, Abigail Calkins Aguirre, Jan Lower, Lori Mattingly Steel, Helen Kemp Zax, Erin Hagar, Erin Barker, and Barbara Crispin. Debbie Gonzales, Annemarie O'Brien, Erin Loomis, Amy Cabrera, Caroline Smalley, Yasmine Kloth, Jill Santopolo, and Sarah Davies, I am lucky to know each one of you.

Many thanks also to my family, of whom I feel quite lucky and proud to be a part: my mom, Patricia Beard; Heidi and John Potterfield; Sam, Anna, and Lily; Troy Beard; Nate, Olivia, and Ella; Jerry and Shirley Stout; Lori and Kirk Thibault; Janie and Jon Mills; Rachel and Alan Thibault; Jeff and Tammy Stout; Josh and Megan; Mary Ann Mundey; Carol Dowling; Kristin Spenser; and Aunt Julie Over.

I consider myself the luckiest of girls to have met my husband, Andy, and to be blessed with our daughter, Opal. All of this is for you and because of you.